Blossom Time

Blossom Time

Joan Smith

LARGE PRINT
Oxford

Copyright © Joan Smith, 1997, 2005

First published in Great Britain 2005
by
Robert Hale Limited

Published in Large Print 2006 by ISIS Publishing Ltd.,
7 Centremead, Osney Mead, Oxford OX2 0ES
by arrangement with
Robert Hale Limited

British Library Cataloguing in Publication Data
Smith, Joan, 1953–
    Blossom time. – Large print ed.
    1. Love stories
    2. Large type books
    I. Title
    813.5'4 [F]

ISBN 0–7531–7493–6 (hb)
ISBN 0–7531–7494–4 (pb)

Printed and bound in Great Britain by
T. J. International Ltd., Padstow, Cornwall

CHAPTER
ONE

A bemused smile played on Rosalind's lips as she sat in the garden of Apple Hill, repairing yet another hem torn loose by Sukey. The beauty of Kent, the orchard of England, was all around her. As the name indicated, Apple Hill grew mainly apples — seventeen varieties. The spring glory of blossom time, when the orchards foamed in white and pearly pink, was past, but in the cutting garden, roses and peonies, their heads heavy with petals, nodded in the sunlight. Their perfume scented the air. It was not the enchantment of her surroundings that caused Rosalind's smile, however. It was the copy of a literary magazine, the *Camena*, which she had received in the post that morning.

Finally seeing her poetry in print was a joy akin to laying eyes on one's firstborn child. And it was not just a single poem, either. The editor, Lord Sylvester Staunton, had devoted a whole section to his new protégée and written a critique himself. He had praised her work's "refined sensitivity", comparing her love of nature to that of William Wordsworth. *Blossom Time* was the title she had chosen for her collection of spring poems, composed last spring and polished over the winter.

Lord Sylvester had discovered things in the poems that she had not known were there. Her "sleep of winter", he said, was a metaphor for not only the dormant plants but for the slumbering soul of mankind in the early eighteenth century. Her transformation of barren branches to leaves and flowers in spring, he opined, was the new romantic renaissance in poetry. Even her frozen apple trees were likened by Lord Sylvester to the story of Persephone and a host of other classical myths, many of which she had never heard of. She had dutifully looked up each one in the library to broaden her knowledge, for like most ladies of her class, she lacked real training in the classics.

She felt the publication and the praise were all because Lord Sylvester had mistaken her for a man. For two years she had sent out poems under her own name, only to have them come thumping back to her as too frivolous for the readers of the various magazines to which she had submitted them. The first time she had used her second name, Frances, changing the e to i, she had met with success — and it confirmed her suspicion that it was her sex that had kept her out of print. Her smile held a tinge of gloating. *Camena* was the most prestigious of all the new literary magazines, and Lord Sylvester had loved her poems.

Wrapped up in her thoughts, she didn't hear Lord Harwell's approach when he came striding through the orchard. He stopped a moment at the edge of the garden; gazing at her, wondering about that smile. It struck him that his neighbor, Rosalind Lovelace, was as pretty as any of the chits he'd left behind in London. It was unusual to see her sitting at her ease in the garden. She was more likely to be bustling off to the vicarage to help with the chores there, or teaching Sukey to ride, or rushing about her brother's estate in the donkey cart, delivering pork jelly to an ailing tenant or blankets and linen to a new mama.

Sunlight filtered through the branches of the primrose bush under which she sat, dappling her face in shadows. Her brown hair, tinged with copper, gave off sparks of light where the sun struck it. When she glanced up and saw him, she gave him a warm smile of welcome. He had never considered Roz beautiful, but she had a liveliness and down-to-earth charm that was better than beauty. Her eyes, he thought, were her best feature. It was unusual to see eyes so green. Usually they had some trace of brown or yellow. Hers were the clear, dark, brilliant green of a holly leaf.

He bowed with playful formality. "Good afternoon, Miss Lovelace," he said.

"Hullo, Harry," she replied, and peered playfully over his shoulder. "Home from London once again without a bride, I see. Another Season wasted."

Lord Harwell lived by the credo "Work hard, play hard, and love hard". He devoted six weeks of each spring to loving and playing hard. The rest of the time he was busy about his estate, Drayton Abbey, producing the best hops in the country and introducing improvements in his herd of Guernseys, with occasional breaks for playing and loving to keep his hand in.

"Not entirely wasted," he said, and picked up the sewing basket by her side and sat down. "I enjoyed a few delightful flirtations."

She looked at him from the corner of her eye. "Getting a bit long in the tooth for flirtations, aren't you?" she chided.

In Rosalind's view, it was past the time when Lord Harwell should marry and settle down. He was the only son; it was his place to sire an heir and train him up to his future role. Harwell featured largely in Rosalind's daydreams, but she had too much barnyard common sense to let dreams color her reality. Harwell was just a friend. When he married, it would be to some fine lady from the tip of the *ton*.

He was one of those dashing rogues too rakish to trust, and too attractive to ignore. His dark good looks were more rugged than handsome. A shock of straight black hair fell over his forehead when he removed his curled beaver and tossed it aside. His broad, square shoulders were covered in a well-tailored jacket of blue superfine. In the country, he dispensed with a cravat and wore a comfortable dotted belcher kerchief, but there was no danger of mistaking him for a provincial buck. From head to toe he was the epitome of elegance. His barbering was excellent, his top boots gleamed, and his buff trousers were spotless.

He had the reputation of a flirt, but he had never had a flirtation with his closest neighbor. He was too wise a bird to foul his own nesting area. Over the years, he and Rosalind had settled into an undemanding friendship, like a couple of gentlemen. He had been very helpful,

4

especially to Dick, when Mr Lovelace had died five years before.

"I expect we are reaching that age where we should bite the bullet and settle down," he agreed.

"We?" she asked, lifting a shapely eyebrow in mock dudgeon. "You can give me close to a decade, Harry. I have not yet hit the quarter-century mark." She was twenty-four, like her twin brother, Dick.

"You can't be far from it. Face it, Roz, bachelorhood stares us both in the face." The words were hard, but spoken in a light manner.

She lifted the tail of her skirt slightly and said, "This, for your information — though I should hardly think you of all people need be told — is a skirt, milord, not buckskins or pantaloons."

His eyes skimmed over her yellow dimity gown with a white bib. As usual, her only effort at adornment was a little cameo medallion. The tail of her petticoat showed beneath the skirt. A perfectly plain muslin affair. "And a very . . . serviceable skirt it is, ma'am. Did I mention petticoats trimmed with lace are all the crack in London this Season?"

"We were discussing my skirt. No need to inquire how you have become familiar with ladies' petticoats."

He gave a rakish grin. "Ask away!"

Rosalind ignored this, as she always ignored his broad talk, unless it passed the bounds of acceptable behavior. "The point is, ladies are not bachelors."

"A thousand pardons. Would it lessen the sting if I had said spinster?" She smiled, when he expected to see a frown. "You've gone and found yourself a beau!" he exclaimed. "I am disappointed with you. I thought you and I would dodder into senility together, Roz. Who is he?"

"Don't be ridiculous."

"A lady don't smile like a moonling when she's accused of being a spinster if she knows there's a grain of truth in it."

"There's more to life than marriage. But I don't have to tell you that. No need to remind a bee of honey."

"This goes from bad to worse! Setting up as a light-skirt, Roz? But how intriguing!" He grinned rakishly. "You might have saved me a trip to London if you had let me know."

He didn't expect her to blush, nor did she. Neither did she mount her high horse and give him a scold. Miss Lovelace had never had a Season, but neither was she a girl. At four and twenty, she had had her share of beaux and knew something of the world.

"Pray lift your mind — and speech — from the gutter if you can," she said in a perfectly bland voice, and picked up the needle to resume her chore.

"Come now, who is he?" Lord Harwell persisted.

To show her lack of interest in this topic, she said, "Did you bring any company back with you, Harry?"

"No. Who is he?"

"I thought your Uncle Ezra might have come. He usually does after the Season, does he not?"

"I was fortunate. He has the gout. He's staying at the London house to be near his doctor. Whoever he is —"

"Don't you know who his doctor is?"

"Whoever *your* *lover* is, you have my blessing."

"That, of course, weighs heavily on my mind," she said ironically. "And it is not very flattering that you would happily hand me over to any old hedge bird, sight unseen."

"*Au contraire!* It is a compliment on your good taste and common sense. You would not toss your round bonnet at anyone ineligible. I'm sure he is an unexceptionable old hedge bird."

"That demeaning 'round bonnet' was quite unnecessary, Harry. I'll have you know my new spring bonnet has a six-inch poke."

"The new height is eight inches. Er, what did you say your fellow's name is?"

She gave him an arch smile. "I didn't say," she replied, and plunged her needle neatly into the skirt of Sukey's gown.

"A secret admirer? How . . . adolescent."

"No admirer at all. At least not in the way you mean," she said, thinking of Lord Sylvester.

Harwell noticed the soft smile that touched her lips and made the echo of a dimple in her left cheek. A breeze shifted the branch above her, and a shaft of sunlight turned her hair to fire. He gazed a moment, watching the play of sunlight on her cheeks.

"I repeat, a lady don't wear that particular expression if she isn't in love."

A smile lit the green eyes that glanced up from her sewing. "Seen it often, have you, Harry?"

"Only occasionally, and never on a lady I had any wish to marry. If you've settled for a lover, you can do better than whoever he is."

"You don't know who he is."

"I know he ain't me."

"That is ungrammatical, also highly egotistical."

"So you *do* have a lover! I knew it! You've as well as admitted it."

"One admits to a fault, or an error. There would be nothing amiss in my having a beau. If I had one, which I don't, you would be one of the first to know."

"Then what is making you — glow?" he asked, hesitating over the last word. He had never seen Roz so radiant.

"Springtime, I expect," she prevaricated.

She wanted to shout her triumph from the treetops, but discretion kept her silent. As her poetry had been published under a masculine name, she meant to continue the hoax until she was established. Harry had too broad a field of friends and acquaintances to trust him with the secret. She was proud of her work, but it was not something that he would be interested in. As Harwell's friend and neighbor for as long as she could remember, she had never seen him read a poem, or mention one. His reading consisted of the journals, the farming magazines, and for light entertainment, the racing and gentlemen's magazines.

Harry tilted his head, raised one eyebrow, and gave her a quizzing glance. Before he could say more, the air was shattered by a yelp, and a child came hurtling like a bullet onto his lap. The child was closely followed by a barking spaniel, who added his dusty paws to Lord Harwell's spotless buckskins. The child was Rosalind's young sister, Sukey. A tousle of golden curls tickled his chin. As she turned her head, she smote him with a pair of big blue eyes and a dimpled smile. Sukey had her papa's coloring.

"Harry! Did you bring me a present from London?" she asked. "You said you would. You promised."

"Mind your manners, Sukey," Rosalind said. "A lady does not cadge gifts."

Harry said mischievously, "The sort who throw themselves on a fellow's lap do, actually."

"We are speaking of *ladies*, Lord Harwell."

He fished in his pockets but came up empty-handed. "Ali, I must have left it at home," he lied, trying to remember what he had promised her.

"What is it? Is it sugarplums?" Sukey asked eagerly.

"That's it." He'd pick some up next time he was in the village.

Rosalind just shook her head. "I don't know which of you is worse — Sukey for begging, or you for promising and then forgetting."

Sukey scowled. "Don't forget next time."

She scrambled down from his knee. As she reached to stroke Sandy's ears, Rosalind noticed she had torn yet another hem. "I have half a mind to put her in trousers," she said. "That is the second hem she's torn this week. It's pelting after that dog that does the mischief."

"What you need is a kitten, Sukey," he said. "I shall bring you one tomorrow."

Rosalind gave him a knowing look. "That mangy brindle cat of yours has been blessed with another

9

litter, has she? Don't try to palm them off on us. We already have six kittens in the barn."

"I want another kitten," Sukey said.

"One of mine is snow white," Harry said, directing his temptation at Sukey. "A pretty little ball of white fur that just fills the palm of your hand. I call her Snow Drop."

"It would be a *her*," Rosalind murmured.

"Oh, Roz, can I have her?" Sukey begged. "Can I have Snow Drop? I don't have a white kitten."

"Of course you can." Harwell glinted a triumphant smile at Rosalind. "Your sister wouldn't be so cruel as to deprive you of a snow white kitten."

"Especially when she has already been deprived of the sugarplums she was promised," Roz retorted. "Very well. I daresay there are plenty of mice in the barn to go around. But just one kitten, mind."

"Sukey shall have her sugarplums as well — as soon as I get into the village."

"Thanks, Harry," Sukey said. Sandy went yelping after some new scent, with Sukey flying at his heels.

"Where is Sukey's nanny?" Lord Harwell asked, when they were alone again.

"Miss Axelrod has accepted an offer of marriage."

"Another spinster has accomplished the impossible. Marvelous how you old — older ladies can find someone to slip a set of manacles on."

"And Miss Axelrod all of nineteen. It is really a wonder she had the strength to do it. She left us in May. It is no matter. She was really only a nursery maid. Sukey requires a governess. She will be six this month. Time to get her nose to the grindstone."

Rosalind's smile was tinged with sadness to think of Sukey growing up. Mrs Lovelace had died giving birth to Sukey. At that time, Rosalind had taken over as mistress of Apple Hill, and as stand-in mother to Sukey. It had thrown Rosalind's life into turmoil. At eighteen she had been betrothed to Sir Lyle Standish. The year of mourning had delayed the marriage. Before the year was over, Mr Lovelace had died of a chill. The romance with Lyle might have withstood one year of mourning; it was not up to a second. She had regretfully given him his congé. Within the year, he had married the local schoolmistress.

Dick, her twin brother, had been about to go up to Oxford that autumn. Instead, he had been pitched, quite unprepared, into the role of master of a large estate. It had taken his and Rosalind's combined efforts, with ample help from Harwell, to run the place. Dick was not at all sorry to miss out on university. He was not bookish, but he was very good about estate matters. It was soon clear he had no head for ciphering, though. The keeping of the books and the management of the house fell to Rosalind. There hadn't seemed to be much time to find another husband.

Dick had derived his comfort from riding, hunting, shooting, and those masculine activities of his class. He had recently found himself a lady and was engaged. Rosalind had struck up a friendship with the vicar and his wife and become active in church doings. Her solace, when she was alone, was reading, which soon

11

led to trying her own hand at writing. She had always liked poetry and nature. She wrote about the beauty of the changing seasons. It was a diversion, something happy and peaceful to think about, to keep the blue devils at bay when she was alone.

Harwell, watching as these thoughts left a trace of sadness on her face, said, "Haven't brought him up to scratch yet, eh?"

She jerked back to attention. "What? Oh, still harping on my imaginary beau? No, I was just thinking how quickly time passes."

"Very true. Time flies when one is with a pretty lady. I am referring, of course, to Sukey," he added mischievously, as a light flush colored her cheek. He rose and stretched his long arms. "I must be off for a word with my bailiff. I'll bring the cat tomorrow."

"Harry! You said kitten!"

"Right, the kitten. Snow Flake."

"Snow *Drop*, you wretch! And she had better be pure white."

"I'll touch her up with talcum powder before I come," he said, and slanting his curled beaver at a dashing angle over his right eye, he left, laughing.

It was good to be back home. He wondered who Roz's beau could be. She had worn a very sly face as she denied his existence, so of course, she had someone in her eye. Whoever he was, he was making a wise choice. Roz was a fine, level-headed lady.

As he proceeded through the meadow toward the abbey, his thoughts turned to estate matters.

In London, Lord Brampton had alerted him that old Anglesey was giving up farming. Too old for it, and no son to carry on. Anglesey had a fine line of milchers. He would pick up a couple for breeding purposes. Pity Anglesey had never married. It was time he began to keep an eye out for a wife himself, come to that. Maybe next Season would throw up a likely prospect.

CHAPTER
TWO

Rosalind's heart gave a little leap when she was handed the post at breakfast the next morning. She recognized the spidery writing on her one letter. It was from Lord Sylvester. When she tore it open and read the note, her leaping heart plummeted.

"Good God! He's coming here!" she exclaimed.

"Who? Uncle Ralph?" Dick asked, glancing up from his gammon and eggs. Dick and Rosalind were not usually taken for twins by strangers, but one could see at a glance they were related. They shared their late mama's brown hair and tall build. In Dick, Mrs Lovelace's deep green eyes were faded to hazel, while his complexion was akin to a hazelnut from his outdoor activities. He was usually mistaken for Rosalind's younger brother.

"He's due for his annual holiday," he continued. "Put him in the yellow suite, send up a case of claret, and you'll never know he's here."

"Not Uncle Ralph! Lord Sylvester!"

"Who the deuce is Lord Sylvester? Oh, that magazine fellow who's printed your poems? Jolly good. It will be nice for you to meet him in person."

"No, it won't, Dick. Have you forgotten he thinks I'm a man? You'll have to pretend you're Francis Lovelace. Will you do it?" She knew even as she spoke the words that Dick couldn't fool a child, let alone a scholarly gentleman like Lord Sylvester. But who else was there to do it?

"A man? How can he think that?"

"I told you, I called myself Francis, with an *i*. You'll have to be Francis — just for the visit. Don't do much talking."

"Me pose as a poet?" he cried in horror. "A man scribbling verse. I couldn't do it. I'd be the laughing-stock of the parish if it ever got about."

"It won't get about. And Lord Byron is hardly a laughing-stock."

"Your verses, m'dear sis, ain't Byron's. He don't write the sort of rubbish you do about love and flowers and moonlight. He writes about corsairs and such exciting stuff. Besides, this Sylvester fellow has already published the verses. The magazine is out. He can't take it back."

"He won't publish any more if he knows I'm a lady."

"That don't seem fair," Dick said, frowning. "When is he coming?" he added, with a smirk. She knew from his expression that he was thinking what a good jest it would be to lead Lord Sylvester on, behaving like a mincing, capering dandy.

"Today. This afternoon."

"How long is he staying?"

"Only an hour or so, I should think. It is just a running visit. He mentions he is on his way home to

Astonby to visit his family and will dart in to meet me. I shall ask him to tea."

"Pity Uncle Ralph ain't here. He can prose on for hours about iambic pentameters and sonnets and ballads. I'll do it, but mind I can't waste much time. I have to see my man of business in town today. You'd best show me what you've written again. One of the verses was about my apple trees, I recall. That reminds me, the pippins must be sprayed. I saw greenflies in the orchard yesterday."

This speech was enough to tell Rosalind her brother wasn't up to the job of fooling Lord Sylvester. "I wonder if I could fool him into thinking I'm a man if I wore trousers," she said, frowning into her teacup.

"Gudgeon!" Dick said bluntly. "He's a man, you're a lady. You might bat your lashes at him. What do you think they're for? And wear a decent gown, show a bit of skin. Gents like that. Feed him some of Cook's cream tarts. I'll serve my best claret. We'll have him eating out of your hand."

"I wonder if it would work," she said. "He might be an elderly gentleman. He sounds very scholarly."

"Dash it, he ain't blind or dead, is he? It's worth a try at least."

As there was no one she could put forth as Francis Lovelace, she decided to do as Dick suggested, and try to flirt Lord Sylvester into accepting her as a female poet. She spoke to Cook about serving her finest tea, then darted abovestairs to refashion a gown that would give some suggestion of her female charms without making her blush. She also had her hair done up in

16

papers and applied a strawberry mask to brighten her cheeks. Rosalind was quite an adept with her needle. She chose her green sprigged muslin and lowered the neckline two inches. She took luncheon in the nursery with Sukey, as she did not wish to appear at the table with her hair in papers.

"Can I meet Sylvester?" Sukey asked, ladling a spoonful of mulligatawny into her mouth.

"You may make a brief visit, but you mustn't call him Sylvester, Sukey. Call him Lord Sylvester, or milord."

"I don't call Harry, Lord Harry."

"Harry is a good friend. Actually you should call him Lord Harwell."

Sukey paid no heed to this. "Can I have papers in my hair, Roz?"

"You don't need them. Your hair is almost too curly already."

"Harry didn't bring my kitten," Sukey said, slipping a slice of ham into her pinafore pocket for Sandy.

"He will, eventually."

As soon as lunch was over, Rosalind bustled back to her bedchamber to fashion her toilette. At three o'clock she was sitting in state in the Green Saloon with a shawl wrapped around her shoulders to hide the daring top of her gown; her hair was artfully arranged in a loose knot of curls, with a rosebud stuck into it. She would remove the shawl if Lord Sylvester was younger than fifty, and if he seemed unhappy that she was a lady.

At a quarter after three, Dick said he could no longer delay his trip to town and left. When he returned an hour later, Lord Sylvester still had not arrived. Rosalind's expression was tinged with ennui. The rosebud in her hair had begun to wilt.

"What, not here yet?" Dick asked. "He ain't coming. Let us have our tea."

"No, let us wait until four-thirty," Rosalind parried.

Before the quarter hour was up, they heard a commotion out front, the pounding of hooves and rattle of wheels. Rosalind darted to the window for her first glimpse of Lord Sylvester. From his critique of her work, she expected to see an older, slightly dry scholar. The gentleman who stepped down from the crested carriage was a tall, slender young dandy with a posy attached to the top of his walking stick. The sun shone on blond curls that reminded her of Sukey. He looked to be nineteen or twenty years of age. He stood a moment, looking all around the park, examined the façade of the house, then threw out his arms and lifted his face to the sun.

"That can't be Lord Sylvester!" she exclaimed.

Dick had gone to stand behind her. "There don't seem to be anyone else stepping out of the rig," he said. "He's coming to the door. Must be him. Foppish-looking fellow, ain't he?"

"Do you think so?" she asked in surprise. "I thought he looked charming."

They rushed back to their seats and were apparently chatting unconcernedly when Lord Sylvester Staunton was announced. Dick spared a derisive glance at his mincing step, his tight-fitting jacket and cream buckskins. Nor did he much care to see a lady's coiffure on a man, but the fellow was handsome enough and very gentlemanly. Rosalind, gazing at his blond curls, was not reminded of Sukey this time, but of a Renaissance painting. She thought his smile was very sweet, and when he opened his lips, his voice was like music. Even when he lifted a quizzing glass to his eye and turned it slowly from Dick to her, she was not put off. The elegant way he curved his wrist brought a whiff of London to the provincial saloon.

"Madam," he said, making a leg. Then he turned to Dick. "And you, sir, must be Francis Lovelace. May I say I am honored, deeply honored, to make your acquaintance."

Dick made a jerky bow and looked uncomfortable. "Mutual, I'm sure. Come in, Lord Sylvester. Have a seat. My sister Rosalind was just about to call for tea. Perhaps a glass of wine first. A dry business, driving." He shouted to Rucker for the tea, then poured the wine and went to the sofa.

Lord Sylvester glided like a zephyr across the saloon and perched daintily on the corner of the sofa nearest to Dick. "Everyone is raving about your poetry, Mr Lovelace. Such charming imagery, such lyric grace," he said, accepting the claret. A sip told him it was an excellent vintage. "I feel quite like an explorer discovering a new continent. Like stout Cortez, silent upon his peak in Darien staring at the Pacific. Only it should have been Balboa, of course. Poor Keats. But then he is a product of the bluecoat school, you must know, not Eton or Harrow. I lay the blame in Leigh Hunt's dish. He ought to have caught the error."

Dick stared at the man as if he had suddenly begun to spout Greek. He looked at Rosalind, frowned, and said to Lord Sylvester, "What error?"

"I am referring to Keats's poem in the *Examiner* last December. Why, it ought to have been Balboa. He discovered the Pacific Ocean."

"Serves him right for putting history into a poem. Not the place for it in my opinion. It's bad enough in prose, but to lumber poetry with it!"

Lord Sylvester had come expecting to find a provincial with effete pretentions, and was surprised to discover what he immediately recognized as an unaffected country squire. He was delighted. The man was an original — the exterior of a rustic hiding a soul of pure artistry under an ill-cut jacket. And handsome besides, with shoulders like a barn door. London would be at his feet! The reputation of *Camena* would be made.

"Not what a true poet like yourself would do, Mr Lovelace," Sylvester said, bowing.

"Afraid there's been a bit of a mix-up," Dick said. "I ain't Francis Lovelace. She is." He tossed his head in Rosalind's direction.

Lord Sylvester was silent a moment as his dreams crashed and shattered around him. A lady! He had been conned by a provincial miss! He'd be the laughing-stock of London. His nose pinched. "I see," he said, then added with a cool smile to Rosalind, "How delightful."

"A misunderstanding," Rosalind said. She decided it was time to unwrap herself from her shawl and let it fall around her waist. "My name is Frances, with an e. It must have been my handwriting — perhaps I inadvertently spotted the page above the e. I was thrilled when you accepted my poetry, Lord Sylvester." Her eyelashes fluttered in double time. "Only a gentleman of your scholarly reputation would dare to praise a lady's work, to place it on a par with gentlemen's writing. But that is the sort of bold initiative we have come to expect from *Camena*."

This line of talk went down very well with Lord Sylvester, who had a taste for the butter boat. He began to think that he might make something of Miss Lovelace after all. She was rather pretty — that couldn't hurt. He liked the notion that only he would be so daring as to puff up a lady. When the truth was revealed, he must let it be known that he had realized she was a lady from the beginning.

"*Camena*. What does the word mean?" she asked. "I could not find it in any of my reference works."

"You are not the first to inquire, Miss Lovelace," he said, in quite a civil way. "It is the Latin equivalent of Muse. Muse, of course, is Greek. The word is done to death. I had thought of using the word Erato, the Muse of poetry, but then it tends to be confused with errata and, of course, Eros, laying the name open to coarse jests. I would not want my magazine to be mistaken for some bawdy thing. In the end, I went with *Camena*."

"Roz is greatly interested in such things," Dick said. "A regular bluestocking."

"Oh, hardly that!" she objected. "But I do feel I have learned a great deal from your critiques in *Camena*, milord. I was thrilled that a gentleman of your pre-eminence found my poems worth looking into."

The more she talked, the better he liked her. The tea tray arrived and she poured, making a great show of asking how he took his tea, and would he care to try Cook's pastries.

"Roz is up on all the latest writing," Dick threw in, thinking to puff her off. "She's not content with simple country pleasures. Quite the dasher is Roz."

Lord Sylvester listened with rising hopes. He saw that Miss Lovelace was no deb. She had been out and about for a few years. The word "dasher" raised his hopes for some serious flirtation, preferably away from her home parish. London, for choice. He was soon "confessing" that he had suspected a lady was behind the poems from the beginning.

"Truth to tell," he lied, "it is half the reason I came down to see you. I was hoping that you would have something we might put out in our autumn issue. After its publication in early September would be a good time to introduce you to the literati in London, when interest is at its peak."

"Oh, I should like it of all things, milord!" she cried. Her cheeks were flushed with pleasure and her green eyes glowed.

Lord Sylvester drew out a cloisonné snuffbox, lifted a pinch between his thumb and forefinger, and applied it to his nose. He flickered his handkerchief over his nostrils to dispel any lingering residue but did not sneeze.

"And London will adore you, Miss Lovelace," he said, gazing flirtatiously into her eyes. "One item is not yet clear to me, however. With such a charming and redolent name as Rosalind, why did you sign your letter Frances? I notice Mr Lovelace calls you Roz."

"Frances is my second name," she said, racking her brain for a better excuse. "I thought it sounded more . . . er, serious than Rosalind."

Lord Sylvester studied her a moment, then his thin lips opened in a conspiratorial smile. "You don't fool me, Miss Lovelace," he charged. "You were playing Ganymede."

"Oh, indeed, I —" She stopped in confusion. What was Ganymede? It sounded vaguely familiar, but she could not recall where she had read it.

"And who else but a Rosalind should pose as a gentleman to gain her end?" Sylvester continued. "I am referring, of course, to Shakespeare's *As You Like It*, in which the fair Rosalind assumes the guise of a man, Ganymede. It is an excellent jest. Superb. I shall mention our clever stunt, using a gentleman's name to coerce my readers into taking your work seriously. We shall be quite open and honest about it. It was a hoax. Nay, we shall be aggressive in our attack. Ladies' talents have been overlooked for too long. They will be green with envy at the *Edinburgh Review*."

It did not seem the proper moment to mention that *Miss* Lovelace's poems had been rejected by *Camena*, as well as other literary magazines. Rosalind noticed

23

that her stunt had become our stunt, and as the visit continued, it became entirely Lord Sylvester's stunt. She was so relieved he had accepted her that she just smiled her agreement with everything he said until the tea was consumed. She noticed that Lord Sylvester ate practically nothing, perhaps to allow his tongue freedom to wag.

Rosalind enjoyed the visit. The corner of Kent where she lived was thin of literary folk. Lord Sylvester knew everyone famous and had amusing anecdotes about them to relate. He was also undeniably knowledgeable about literary matters. He was a great talker, but a fatiguing one, for he expected praise for his ideas, laughter for his slightest jest, and scorn to match his disparagement of any other literary review than *Camena*.

He had been in the saloon for only forty-five minutes, but it seemed longer. When he mentioned leaving, Dick leapt from his chair like a grasshopper to accompany him to the door. Rosalind did not urge Lord Sylvester very strenuously to remain, although she had enjoyed his company.

"Must you go so soon?" she said politely, assuming a positive answer.

Before Lord Sylvester could reply, the door knocker sounded, and before Rucker, the butler, could get to the door, Lord Harwell's hearty voice was heard. After one knock, he had let himself in. "It's only me, Roz. I've brought Sukey's kitten."

Of all the people who might have called, Harwell was the last one she wished to present to Lord Sylvester. At no point did their interests meet. Lord Sylvester's only concerns appeared to be literary, while Harwell thought less of literature than of a spot of lint on his sleeve. It would be like struggling through a bramble bush to make conversation with the two of them at once. And on top of it, she did not want Harwell to know she had turned poet. She clenched her lips into a tight smile and waited.

CHAPTER
THREE

The white kitten Lord Harwell held cradled in his arms was strangely at odds with his rakish appearance. "As if Zeus came calling with a rose in his hand in lieu of a thunderbolt" was Lord Sylvester's first impression. Harwell's opinion of Sylvester was equally unsettling. Surely this male milliner was not the gent who brought that glow to Roz Lovelace's face? He was too young, too foppish, not up to her weight — though a very pretty fellow, to be sure. Rosalind's obsequious behavior toward the young whelp left no doubt this was the man responsible for her new glow. Neither gentleman betrayed any of his feelings when Rosalind introduced them.

"I believe we have rubbed shoulders at Brooks's, milord," Sylvester said, making an exquisite bow.

"Very likely," Harwell agreed. He switched the kitten to his left arm and pumped Sylvester's hand. "You are Dunston's younger son, if I am not mistaken?"

"Just so. I believe my older brother, Lord Moffat, has the honor of your acquaintance."

"Indeed, I have known Moffat forever. We were at Eton together a hundred years ago. How is he? I haven't seen him about London recently."

"He is married with two sons now, living at Astonby. He is gradually taking over management of the estate. Papa is poorly, you must know."

"I am sorry to hear it."

Rosalind was glad that Sylvester acquitted himself creditably in this exchange. She wished he would now rise and leave, before anything was said of the reason for his visit. What excuse could she give Harry for it? Lord Sylvester lost his way and stopped for directions was the best she could come up with. She was aware of Harwell's dark eyes raking her. That frown growing between his eyes indicated curiosity.

Harwell's frown had less to do with Lord Sylvester than with Rosalind's appearance. When had she begun sticking flowers in her hair and wearing low-cut gowns? Even at the local balls and assemblies she was always very modest in her toilette. In her new style, and with that simpering smile on her face, she reminded him of a light-skirt. It annoyed him to no small degree. It seemed inconceivable that this young popinjay had made her so far forget her sensible self.

These thoughts flashed through his mind in seconds. When he spoke, he said, "I didn't realize you knew Miss Lovelace. I haven't met you here before, have I?" His friendly tone encouraged Sylvester's confidence.

"Until today, our acquaintance has been by correspondence only, purely professional," Sylvester said, with a conspiratorial smile at Rosalind. "I dare to hope we have taken the initial steps toward friendship over the past delightful hour."

Harwell's eyebrows rose an inch. "In what field of endeavor have you turned professional, Roz?" he inquired. "Setting up as a mender of prayer books?" His curiosity was rampant, and his speech, which always bordered on the brusque, sounded more angry than curious.

Sylvester blinked in astonishment. "Milord! Don't tell me you are Miss Lovelace's neighbor and are not aware that we devoted four pages of the current issue of *Camena* to her works! She is the next poet laureate. I use the word in its true sense of being wreathed in laurels, honored above her peers, not appointed by His Majesty to spin off court odes on order, like that doddering fool Southey. Walter Scott had the good sense to turn the post down."

Harwell's jaw fell open. "Roz, a poet?" he exclaimed, and stared at her as if she had been pronounced a contortionist, or a bearded lady. "What do you write about? Mending the seat covers in the church? Stirring up the annual batch of marmalade?"

Green fire shot from her eyes, glaring him to a stunned silence. He hadn't seen her so angry since the day he jokingly accused her of trying to seduce the vicar.

Before she could retaliate in words, Sylvester took up the cudgels in her defense. His chivalry sent a little thrill through her, and created a new sort of interest in this young dandy. He was not all that young either, to judge by his speech.

"The mind needs ease for contemplation to create great literature, milord," he said, with an air of gentle reproof. "It has been my experience that it is those engaged in simple pursuits who create the true masterpieces. Wordsworth, for example, strolling through the woods with his sister, and enlightening us and posterity as to his sublime feelings. Think of Thomas Gray. The greatest excitement of his mature writing years was his remove from Peterhouse across the street to Pembroke Hall — and it took a fire to move him that far. Yet there are lines in the *Elegy* so beautiful they make grown men weep." He gazed into the distance and blinked away an unshed tear.

"If a dull life is the prerequisite for great poetry, then I am sure you will do admirably," Harwell said with a mocking bow in Rosalind's direction.

"The hurly-burly of a Season would only dilute Miss Lovelace's originality," Sylvester insisted. "She does plan to visit London soon, however. The other poets are on thorns to meet her, since her triumphant appearance in *Camena*."

Harwell's sharp eyes turned to Roz at this announcement. "Indeed! I have heard nothing of this visit," he said.

"We have just begun to discuss it," she replied.

"Ah yes, a week in London will require a deal of discussion," he said, chewing back a grin.

"Longer than a week, I hope!" Sylvester exclaimed. "I am anticipating a month at least, perhaps two. I shall begin looking about for a flat for you as soon as I return to Town, Miss Lovelace."

"My London house is empty in the summer, except for a few servants and Aunt Margaret. Oh, and Uncle

Ezra at the moment," Harwell said. "You are welcome to stay there, Roz. Aunt Margaret can accompany you about."

"That's very kind of you, Harry," she said, with a thin smile, "but I am hardly at that age where I require a chaperon."

"I have been anticipating the pleasure of being Miss Lovelace's cicisbeo," Sylvester said with a glinting smile at Harwell. Why was the fellow jealous of him? Was there something afoot between this unlikely pair?

Harwell's frown grew deeper at every speech. "When are we to see the magnum opus?" he inquired.

"I believe I have a spare copy of the current issue of *Camena* in my rig," Sylvester said. "I shall give you one before I leave, but we do not call the *Blossom Time* poems Miss Lovelace's magnum opus, merely a prelude to greater things to come." He went on to speak of *Camena*, and his stunt in pretending Miss Lovelace's poems had been composed by a gentleman.

Lord Harwell had only a minimal interest in the details. When Sylvester stopped to draw breath, Harwell said to Rosalind, "Where is Sukey? As you see, I brought Snow Drop for her."

"Snow Drop?" Sylvester said. "Snowflake, surely. Raindrop but snowflake is the usual terminology."

Harwell's sigh suggested his lack of interest in semantics.

Before long, Sukey came barrelling into the saloon. Her hem had torn loose once again. A sunbonnet hung down her back, held on by its ribbon. Her tousled curls bounced in all directions. The soiled condition of her pinafore suggested that she had been playing in the stable, or perhaps in a ditch. Ignoring everyone and everything else in the room, she bolted straight for Snow Drop and snatched her into her arms to kiss her.

"Thanks, Harry!" she exclaimed. "Did you bring the sugarplums too?"

"Er . . . not yet," he said, darting a guilty look at Rosalind.

Sylvester watched with his eyebrows lifted to his hairline. Once Sukey had examined the kitten's entire body and said in an accusing way that the kitten wasn't perfectly white, her feet and belly were gray, she deigned to look around the room and discovered Lord Sylvester.

"Who are you?" she demanded.

"Lord Sylvester, this is my young sister, Sukey," Rosalind said. "You must excuse the way she looks. She is a great tomboy, I fear."

"Should you not be in the classroom, young lady?" Sylvester inquired.

"My nanny got married. We had her wedding dinner here. I drank a glass of wine. I'm on holidays now. When I get a governess, I'm going to learn to read."

"Learn to read? How old are you, Miss Sukey?"

"Five and some more months."

"I was reading at three. At five and a half I was well on my way in Latin and Greek."

Sukey wrinkled up her brow and studied him a moment. "I'm a girl," she said. "I only have to learn to read."

She walked to the tea tray, scooped up a handful of macaroons, and stuffed them in her pocket. She turned an accusing eye on Rosalind. "You didn't tell me Cook had made macaroons. You know they're my favorite." On this bold speech, she turned and strode from the room, with Snow Drop tucked under her arm. In a moment the front door was heard to slam.

"An original," Lord Sylvester said, in a voice that displayed his disapproval, and his gentlemanly restraint in not giving tongue to it.

He rose and began making his bows all around. "Could you suggest the best inn at Croydon, Lovelace?" he said to Dick. "I believe I shall stay the night and return tomorrow. Miss Lovelace and I have a great many things to discuss." He turned to Rosalind. "We must give some thought to those poems for the autumn issue of *Camena*, and set on a date for your visit to London. I shall want to arrange a dinner party and a few outings. I begin to think September is leaving it a bit late."

Dick felt he ought to invite Lord Sylvester to stay at Apple Hill, but he had not the least desire to have to listen to the fellow prose on all evening about *Camena*, as if it were the Holy Grail.

"The Greenman is —" He began, only to be interrupted by Rosalind.

"We would be honored if you would stay —"

Before the invitation left her lips, Lord Harwell spoke. "Might I have the honor of your company, Lord Sylvester? We have rather a fine library at the Abbey.

Some original Spenser manuscripts you might want to have a look at," he added enticingly.

Lord Sylvester was fully alive to the honor of an invitation to visit Drayton Abbey, one of the finest estates in England. He knew, as well, that Lord Harwell was the tip of the *ton*. It occurred to him that he might get Harwell to dig into his deep pockets to invest in *Camena*, whose finances were by no means solid.

"Very kind of you, milord," he said, smiling. Then he turned back to Rosalind. "May I do myself the honor of calling on you this evening, Miss Lovelace, if you are not otherwise occupied?"

"I am free," she said, with some eagerness. Not so much for his company as to get him away from Harwell. Why had Harry invited him? He had no use for gentlemen like Lord Sylvester. Her fear was that Harry would in some manner give Sylvester a disgust of her. Those remarks about mending the church seats and making marmalade were made in a mean spirit that was unlike Harry. Or was she imagining things? Perhaps Sylvester's brother, Lord Moffat, was a good friend of Harry's.

Harwell said, "Or better, why don't you and Dick come to the Abbey and dine with us there, Roz?"

Sylvester's face burst into smiles of approbation. "Too kind, milord. Really this is demmed civil of you. I am honored — flattered at your attentions."

"Roz?" Harwell said. She studied him for a moment, trying to gauge what he was up to. He was smiling blandly, but a spark of mischief beamed in his dark eyes. Almost a challenge. She never could resist a challenge.

"Thank you, Harry. I look forward to it. You are free, Dick?"

"Oh, certainly. There is no Parish Council meeting tonight, and no assembly in town. Very happy to go, Harry. I shall perhaps leave a little early and call on Annabelle."

"Bring Annabelle along. Let us make it a party," Harwell said. "That is Lovelace's fiancée we are discussing, Lord Sylvester. Miss Fortescue, a charming lady. I shall invite Lady Amanda Vaughan to even out our numbers."

Both Rosalind and Dick stared to hear Lady Amanda's name mentioned so casually. Harwell had been avoiding this rapacious man-eater's advances forever. The group began to move into the hall. Harwell fell into step with Rosalind a few paces behind the others.

"Why are you doing this?" she demanded in an angry undertone.

"Why, you sound as if you're ashamed of your young beau, Roz. I thought it a good idea to get to know him a little better before you announce the engagement. You recall your chagrin yesterday that I should consign you to just any old hedge bird."

"Lord Sylvester is hardly a hedge bird!"

"No, more like a peacock."

"If you spoil this for me, Harry —"

"My dear idiot! My intention is to help the affair along. The new gown and the wilted rosebud you've stuck into your hairdo are all very well, but Sylvester is a town peacock. You will have to show more than your clavicle to entrap him into an offer."

"It is not an affair or a courtship. And I don't need any help from you."

"No, but I think perhaps Sylvester does. You must have seen Dick has no opinion of him. He might refuse to hand you over."

"This has nothing to do with Dick, or you, or anyone else but me and Lord Sylvester."

"Is that any way to thank me for voluntarily letting Lady Amanda loose in my saloon? I shall be fortunate to get away with my virtue intact."

"You would be a magician to end up with what you do not possess to begin with. I cannot imagine why you are planning to invite *her*."

His lips moved unsteadily. "Afraid of the competition, Roz?"

"Hardly. Lady Amanda does not write poetry, as far as I know."

"Oh, but I meant competition for my body, not Sylvester's mind."

"She is entirely welcome to your body."

"And to Sylvester's as well?" he asked, staring at her. The only emotion he could discern was anger.

Sylvester turned, bowed to Dick, and took his leave of Rosalind. "I shall give you that copy of *Camena* when we meet chez the Abbey," he was heard to say as the gentlemen walked toward their carriages.

"I look forward to it," Harwell lied, as Rucker closed the door.

"Lord Sylvester is quite a chatterbox, ain't he?" was Dick's only comment, before he went to his study.

Rosalind went with a heavy heart to devise a toilette that would not look dowdy beside Lady Amanda's, and still be within the bounds of modesty.

She felt in her bones the evening would be a disaster. As if trying to mix the oil of Sylvester and the vinegar of Harwell were not enough, there would be Dick's fiancée, Miss Fortescue, playing off her airs and graces, and Lady Amanda, casting her lures at all the gentlemen. It would be a perfectly wretched evening, and it was all Harwell's fault.

CHAPTER
FOUR

Rosalind felt the occasion was special enough to wear the new gown she had had made up for the June assembly. Its watered silk was the rich hue of the heart of a Provence rose before it is fully open. As the color and material were rich, she had had it designed simply, aiming for enduring elegance rather than the latest fashion. All her gowns did service for several years. She asked the gardener to bring her an unopened Provence rose to nestle in the side of her bundle of curls. Her mama's diamonds would be overdoing it for a simple dinner party. She wore her own pearls and topped the outfit off with a white fringed shawl.

"So this is the new gown. You look fine as ninepence, Roz," Dick complimented her when she went downstairs to join him.

He had already called for his fiancée and brought Miss Fortescue to Apple Hill to accompany them to Harwell's. The Fortescues were a new family in the neighborhood. Mr Fortescue had retired from a very profitable law practice in London three years before and removed to Croydon. The location was a compromise. His wife and daughter had no taste for the country; they wanted to be near neighbors and the shops. Fortescue wanted to be near enough to the country that he could ride and hunt.

His daughter and only child was now quite an heiress, which, in Rosalind's view, was the young lady's chief attraction. Even that had its obverse side, as it inclined her to think very highly of herself. For the rest, she was a redhead with cabbage green eyes, a sharp nose, a sharp head for business, and a sharp tongue. She felt Mr Lovelace had done very well to catch her and her fifteen thousand pounds, with a deal more to come when her papa died. Rosalind never could understand what Dick saw in the wench, but he had never been much involved with any of the local ladies, and as he had found someone he was inclined to marry, his sister was careful not to say a word against his choice.

"Roz," Miss Fortescue said, prancing forward to brush her cheek against her future sister-in-law's. "How charming you look. I was right about the watered silk, was I not? Much better than those dreary gowns you usually wear. Even with that plain cut, the color gives you a bit of life you need at your age. And really those little pearls look quite nice," she said, patting her own splash of glittering diamonds. Her gown was of pomona green satin, embellished with a quantity of lace and ribbons. A brightly patterned shawl of red and white trailed over her arm.

"Shall we go?" she rattled on. "It should be dark enough by the time we reach the Abbey that no one sees the dust on Dick's carriage. He is such a slackard!" she added, smiling tolerantly at her beloved. "I have told him a dozen times that you don't drive a dusty rig to visit a lord, but there. I'm sure if a scold like you cannot make him behave, Roz, a mere fiancée can have no hope of reforming him."

Dick accepted this chastisement in good humor. "Dash it, it's only Harry. He has seen me in dirtier rigs than the one we are driving tonight," he said, and ushered the ladies out the door. As they drove the few miles to the Abbey, Miss Fortescue entertained the company with a recital of what an honor she was conferring on Lord Harwell to grace his table that evening on such short notice.

"I was promised to the Coughlins for dinner," she said. "When the note came, I said to the footman, 'You must tell his lordship I cannot accept.' Imagine sending an invitation on the very day of the party! And late afternoon at that. Shabby, I call it. Then I read further and saw that this heedless fellow was to attend." Dick received a poke in the ribs. "What was a lady to do? Attend the Coughlins' rout without an escort and be mobbed by all the provincials, or humbly submit to do as her lord and master ordered? But I am not complaining. I hope I am not one to quibble at such a little solecism. It is always delightful to visit the Abbey. Who else will be there? Have you heard, Roz?"

"A Lord Sylvester Staunton," Rosalind replied.

"Is he anyone?"

"Lord Dunston's younger son," Dick told her. "Dunston is something high in the government."

"No doubt Papa knows him. *Younger* son. I see. Not the heir, then. Pity. He might have made a beau for you, Roz. You will not want to be under our feet at Apple Hill when Dick and I marry. Not that you would not be welcome! I am only thinking of you. It would not be comfortable for you to live as a pensioner in a house where you were used to being the mistress for so many years."

It was such remarks as this that assured Miss Fortescue the lack of popularity she enjoyed.

"I'm sure the house is big enough for all of us," Dick said, and meant it.

This was no new theme to their conversation. Annabelle was always sure to throw in a reminder that a sister-in-law would be de trop in her house. It was one of the reasons Rosalind was so eager to go to London. She was determined to find another abode before the wedding, which was to take place in the autumn. Her hope was that she would meet some gentleman in London and never have to burden Annabelle's hospitality, except for visits.

Lord Sylvester was the most interesting gentleman she had met in an age. She had no objection to a younger son, nor indeed an untitled gentleman, so long as he was of good family. Sylvester's manners were exquisite, he was handsome, and their mutual love of poetry would be a bond. She closed her ears and gazed out the window as the carriage bowled along through the lengthening shadows.

When it slowed to turn in at the massive stone gates of Drayton Abbey, she looked out at the park. At eventide the sun was sinking low on the horizon, gilding the trees and limning their outlines against the violet sky. The park had not received the attentions of any of the famous gardeners. Neither Capability Brown's nor Repton's improving hand had been busy to devise prospects or a meandering stream, or the requisite groups of three trees — two would not clump — in close proximity. The trees were beautifully scattered at random as nature intended, with stretches of grass between. Two deer looked up in surprise and dashed off, their white scuts visible in the deepening shadows.

As the carriage rounded a curve in the road, the stone walls of the Abbey loomed in the near distance. It had been given a new façade a century before, so that it did not look at first glance like an ancient heap. The façade was long, with rows of identical tall, mullioned windows on two storys. A tower in the center and at both ends rose another story, the central one topped with a spindled balustrade. It seemed the Harwells had always been egotistical. The ancestor who had refashioned the façade had had his initials, E.G., carved in fretted stone atop the central tower. The letters stood out against the paler sky. The family name was Gaunt. The *E*, she had been told, stood for Edward, the traditional Christian name of the eldest son, though she had never heard anyone call Harwell Edward.

"We should have that done at Apple Hill, Dick," Annabelle said.

Rosalind turned to see where she was looking. As she feared, it was at the initials atop the Abbey. Rosalind was relieved that Dick laughed.

"Using initials is all the crack," Annabelle informed them. "I saw in a book a letter Queen Bess had written, and it was signed E.R., for Elizabeth Rex. The Rex means queen."

"Rex means king, don't it?" Dick asked Rosalind.

"I believe the R stands for Regina," Roz replied.

"Oh, was that her family name?" Annabelle said, dismissing the whole conversation to wonder again who else would be dining with them and whether there would be dancing.

They were soon deposited at the oaken door with the massive iron knocker fashioned in the shape of the family crest. It was only when one was inside that any lingering sense of the Abbey's history was felt. The arrogance of the exterior was transformed to quiet serenity within, with touches of elegance that did not overpower the senses. There were no Grecian statues sequestered in their niches, but old tapestries hanging on white walls. A lovely carved prie-dieu and six chairs were the only furnishings in the entrance hall. The prie-dieu was of ancient vintage; Harwell had casually tossed his curled beaver, York tan gloves, and riding crop on the hand rest.

"An odd sort of table," Annabelle said with a *tsk*. "And not even a flower arrangement. What this place needs is a woman's touch."

The sound of Lord Sylvester's fluting voice issued from the saloon. When they were shown in, Rosalind's gaze traveled first to Lord Sylvester. He had changed for evening into a gold velvet jacket that she thought a little too flashy for true elegance, but it looked well with his golden curls. Harwell wore a simple bottle green jacket and dark gray pantaloons. He looked massive and dour beside Sylvester's more brilliant presence.

When she glanced at Harwell's face, she noticed he wore an air of utter ennui that he did not bother to try to conceal. Of course, he would be bored with anything cultural. No doubt it was being rescued from intelligent conversation that brought that smile to his face and caused his warm greeting as he rushed forward to welcome the new arrivals. He made the necessary introductions, wine was served, and while Miss Fortescue subjected Lord Sylvester to a catechism, Harwell got Rosalind aside for some private conversation.

"I was never so glad to see anyone in my life," he said, and wiped his brow.

"I take it that is less a compliment to myself than a disparagement of Lord Sylvester's conversation," she replied, already angry with him.

"Conversation? He doesn't know the meaning of the word. I have been subjected to an hour's monologue on the *Faerie Queene*. Did you know it's about King Arthur, among other heroes? Who would have thought that rousing tale could be made so tedious — in six books? Sylvester was lamenting that the other six never got written, or published — I can well believe it! — or something. No doubt Spenser died of boredom. I don't know how you can tolerate that fellow."

"I have no particular fondness for Spenser."

"I mean Sylvester."

"You invited him — just why you did so is unclear, but having done it, you must be polite."

"Why must I? Is it polite for him to bethump a man with an hour of the *Faerie Queene*?"

"Is it polite for you to ramble on forever about your Guernseys?"

He looked chastened. "Do I ramble? Tell me the next time I do it. I would not knowingly trespass on anyone's patience the way that fellow does. Can the man talk nothing but poetic drivel?"

She reined in her temper. "All things look yellow to the jaundiced eye, Harry."

"I doubt it is my jaundiced eye that makes that jacket so — yellow!"

"What I meant is, to some of us, poetry is not drivel. And there is nothing amiss in Lord Sylvester's jacket. I think it is quite stylish."

"Then it is high time you had that visit to London."

"There is no reason a gentleman need dress like an undertaker when he is out enjoying himself."

He stared at her as if seeing her for the first time. "Good Lord, you're serious! I thought I knew you pretty well, Roz. I had no notion you were — romantical," he said, flinging out his hand in disgust.

"I, on the other hand, always knew you were a philistine, interested in nothing but cows and pigs and whoring around with loose women."

A smile quirked the corner of his lips. "You forgot politics. I once wrote a letter to *The Times*."

"Yes, about cows."

"About enclosures!"

"You just wanted the extra acres as pasture for your herd."

He noticed that her eyes were flashing and her bosom heaving. "Your chest is heaving, Roz," he said, gazing at it with keen interest.

"That is no excuse to stare! I'm sure you've seen many a bosom before."

"Not your bosom, though. That gown you wore this afternoon was a tad risqué as well. When did you start wearing stylish gowns?" he demanded irately.

"When I learned Lord Sylvester was coming to visit," she replied, to annoy him.

"Aha! So you are after him!" Harwell felt a wince of some unpleasant emotion he did not care to identify too closely. It certainly wasn't jealousy. No sane man could be jealous of that popinjay. His masculine pride was injured, perhaps. Roz had never bothered to make herself pretty for him.

"What if I am?" she asked, with a memory of Dick's impending marriage. Harwell's mouth fell open in shock. "I find him quite charming."

"He might be tolerable, when he grows up and learns the difference between a monologue and conversation. He's still wet behind the ears. Living in a world of make-believe. Of course, he's only two and twenty, he tells me. I would have thought eighteen or nineteen was closer to it."

Rosalind had thought he was a little older, perhaps twenty-five, but she didn't intend to let Harwell know it. It was Sylvester's encyclopedic knowledge of poetry that had misled her.

"He is two years younger than I am," she said. "I was not considered a babe in arms last year when you made me help you get rid of Mrs Molson by pretending to be on the edge of an engagement to you. Or two years ago, when you were in London and I arranged the offer to purchase Elder's farm for you. Or five years ago when —"

"I take your point, Roz. I have abused our friendship. I am sorry."

"That's not what I mean! We are discussing my age and Lord Sylvester's. He's not a child."

"Well, he acts like one, and apparently his family knows it. He don't come into his estate for another three years, when he's twenty-five. No doubt that is why he dunned me for a thousand pounds for *Camena*. Foolish name. How is one to know from a name like that that it's about poetry? He's trying to con folks into thinking it's something interesting."

Rosalind was shocked to learn Sylvester was still under his family's guardianship. Harwell studied her with growing astonishment as she gazed across the room at Sylvester, with a look not much short of scheming. "You *are* interested in him!" he charged.

"Yes, as my mentor," she said.

She continued looking at Sylvester, who was just giving Annabelle a lovely setdown.

"One does not indulge in poetry for filthy lucre, Miss Fortescue," he was saying. It seemed Annabelle had inquired how much money was to be made at it. She would! "I do not consider myself a magazine merchant, after all."

"But how do you live?" she asked. "You are only a younger son."

Sylvester looked at her as if she were a worm. "But the younger son of a marquess," he said. "A Staunton is hardly expected to wheel a barrow through the streets, or set up as a solicitor."

Annabelle turned a little pink about the ears and smiled, and said not a word about her papa. Before anyone spoke, the butler appeared at the door to announce the last arrival, Lady Amanda Vaughan.

CHAPTER
FIVE

Lady Amanda was a widow thirty some years of age. Her title was a legacy from her papa, Lord Siberry, who had little but a title to leave his brood. Her fortune was from her late husband, who had owned a string of gaming houses of dubious reputation before he was killed in a duel. Her looks were entirely her own doing, for very little of her natural endowments was now visible.

She had enlivened her mousy brown hair to a pretty Titian, her fading cheeks to a rosy pink, and fed her fulsome curves to repletion in the belief that this made her look attractive. She still dressed in the garish style that had pleased her late husband and the clients of his gaming houses. On that evening she wore a large set of emeralds and a coral gown that hugged her rounded curves like a plaster. She was not unattractive, but her attractions were akin to those of a friendly barmaid or actress. She had a lively brown eye and a warm smile.

"Harry, you old dog!" she said, undulating across the room to place a kiss on his cheek. "Summoning me at the very last minute! I know someone called off, and I am merely here to warm an otherwise empty chair. But there, when you summon, we all run to obey." She made a deep and surprisingly graceful curtsy.

Harwell made some polite excuses to which Lady Amanda did not listen. She was too busy scouring the room for gentlemen. The pickings were exceedingly slim. She knew from long experience that she had no hope with Harry. Dick was engaged. That left only the young dandy in the yellow jacket. She squeezed Harwell's fingers, took his wineglass from him, and hastened across the saloon, waving about, but never slowing her pace until she reached her new quarry.

"Lady Amanda Vaughan," she said, giving his hand a vigorous shake. "I think I recognize that pretty face. Don't tell me!"

When Sylvester recovered from his shock, he ignored her command and gave her his name. "Ah, old Dunston's lad," she said. "Whatever brings you to Drayton Abbey? You don't look like a farmer." A raucous laugh trilled from her lips. "Harwell never entertains anyone but glorified farmers, you must know. He and Farmer George are a pair. I shouldn't be much surprised to see him land one of the royal princesses."

Lady Amanda's name was well known in London. That she had sold up Vaughan's gaming houses for fifty thousand pounds and had no children were the facts that had stuck in Lord Sylvester's mind. He was not tardy to mount his hobby-horse and speak of *Camena*. And Lady Amanda, having run through all the eligible gentlemen in the parish, put on her brightest smile and claimed a great interest in poetry.

She held him captive until dinner was called and ignored Harwell when he came to lead her to the dining room. Harwell shrugged and offered his arm, to Rosalind instead.

"You must look to your laurels, Roz," he said. "Your mentor has got the whiff of money for his magazine. I, it hardly needs saying, did not oblige him with the thousand pounds he tried to dun me for. I would advise you to be deaf to his hints as well."

"He didn't ask me. *Camena* is not the sort of magazine where one pays to have her work published," she said with lofty disdain. "In fact, the magazine paid me a tidy sum." She did not mention the extremely minuscule tidy sum paid. It wasn't the money that drove her.

If Sylvester was courting Lady Amanda as a backer, he was too clever to mention money, but he certainly harped on *Camena* until the table was sick and tired of hearing it.

"Fascinating!" Lady Amanda said, smiling relentlessly between sips and sups. Next to dalliance, food and drink were her main pleasures.

When Sylvester realized that his plate was still full while all about him had cleaned theirs, he applied his fork to a tenderloin of mutton.

"You must come to Merton Hall, Lord Sylvester," Lady Amanda said. "I have a wonderful library there. I bought the place fully furnished from old Lord Dinsmore, you know. He was a literary gentleman, like yourself. He mentioned some original manuscripts of John Donne's love poems. There is half a poem there that he never finished. You might like to publish the fragment in *Camena* as a literary curiosity."

Lord Sylvester was suitably impressed. A previously unpublished Donne fragment would be a coup, and it wouldn't cost him a penny if he played his cards right. Unfortunately, Lady Amanda could give him very little notion what the poem was about. "It is written on the back of a laundry list," was all the poetry lover could tell him.

Throughout dinner, the usually voluble Annabelle Fortescue scarcely spoke, except a few words in a low voice to Dick. She was listening avidly, for she sometimes felt the lack of breeding in her background, never more so than when Lord Sylvester's bright eye had speared her and hinted that a solicitor was no better than a costermonger. Anyone who could insult her like that must be a real gentleman. Lord Harwell never spoke so haughtily.

Three couples were not enough to form even one square, so there was no dancing when the gentlemen joined the ladies after taking their port. And, as no sane person ever sat down to cards with Lady Amanda, who had picked up a bag of sharp tricks from her late husband, conversation had to be the postprandial entertainment. Lord Sylvester sat with Rosalind, discussing her autumn series of poems and her remove to London until the tea tray arrived.

Harwell watched with growing concern and was relieved when Lady Amanda joined them. Sylvester asked Rosalind if he could call on her in the morning, and she graciously agreed, before going to have a few words with her host.

"You must have diverted him from his favorite subject," Harwell said. "You were actually smiling."

"We were discussing my favorite subject: my visit to London."

"Shall I write to my housekeeper to let her know you will be using the house?"

"I think not, but thank you for the offer, Harry. Lord Sylvester's papa owns a set of flats on Glasshouse Street. I am thinking of hiring one of them. As I may be staying for some time, I cannot impose on your hospitality. You use the Grosvenor Square house on and off yourself, and it would look odd if I were staying with a bachelor."

"It could hardly be construed as a love nest! My aunt is always there, and God only knows when I will get Uncle Ezra bounced off."

Rosalind hesitated a moment before answering. "When I said I would be staying for some time, what I meant was that I hope to remove permanently to London."

"Permanently!" Harwell spoke loudly enough to draw the attention of the others, who turned in surprise.

"Lower your voice!" she said.

"But why on earth would you do a thing like that? You have always lived at Apple Hill."

"Yes, as its mistress the past several years. When Dick marries, I shall be reduced to little better than a pensioner. I have some money of my own, enough to hire a flat."

"What of Sukey?"

"She will stay at home and have a governess, of course. There was never any talk of my giving her lessons."

"I think you are behaving rashly. Surely you and Annabelle can rub along without coming to cuffs in a house that size. It has dozens of rooms."

"There speaks the voice of inexperience. And besides," she added with a new twinkle in her eye, "I should love to live in London."

When Lady Amanda's advances became a little hotter than Sylvester could handle, he rose and moved toward Harwell and Rosalind, where he immediately collared the conversation and brought it back to his favorite subject. With nothing but another lecture on poetry to look forward to, the guests began to speak of a busy day on the morrow as soon as the tea had been drunk.

"Lord Sylvester must be fatigued after his trip," Harwell threw in, although his houseguest was by no means inclined to drowsiness. He seemed ready to prose on for hours.

Sylvester and Harwell accompanied the dinner guests to the front door. "What time will be convenient tomorrow, Miss Lovelace?" Sylvester asked.

Harwell listened fretfully. Had this dull scald of an evening not been enough to show Roz what her new fellow was like? Tearing after Lady Amanda for half the time and delivering his screeds the other half. No wonder he was so thin; he didn't even stop talking to eat.

"Elevenish?" Rosalind suggested, with every appearance of eagerness.

"Fine. We'll work out an outline for your autumn poems. You may count on half a dozen pages."

"When will you come to Merton Hall to look at the Donne manuscript, Lord Sylvester?" Lady Amanda asked. "Let us make it tomorrow evening. I have a few appointments during the day." The leer of invitation was in her eyes.

An evening visit was fraught with peril. Sylvester blushed and said, "So kind of you, but I'm afraid I shall be leaving tomorrow afternoon. I am on my way home to Astonby. Papa is not well."

"Pity," she said, and drew him a little away from the others. "I so seldom get an opportunity to meet a poet. I was hoping I might involve myself in some manner in your magazine. Oh, not as a contributor! I fear that is not where my talents are," she added, allowing her wicked eyes to suggest her particular talents. "As an investor, perhaps," she said leadingly. "One likes to do her bit for the arts." This was added to let Sylvester know she did not actually expect any monetary dividends from her investment.

"How very kind! Perhaps I could stay a day longer and drop Papa a note."

"We'll be in touch, then," she said, and patted his fingers familiarly before striding out the door with a predatory smile on her face.

Harwell was thoroughly annoyed with his houseguest. To avoid coming to blows with him, he suggested that Sylvester take this opportunity of viewing his library while he attended to some accounts in his study. Once in the handsome oak-lined room, however, he ignored the thick leather-bound accounts and sat, frowning at a sketch of Drayton Abbey as it had looked before it was confiscated by Henry VIII and given to a previous lord of Harwell. He thought of life at the hall without Rosalind living nearby, and the frown grew deeper.

He would miss her. She was as knowledgeable as any gentleman about estate matters and had always taken a keen interest in his doings — commiserating with him during his troubles, rejoicing at his triumphs, and aiding him out of his personal difficulties, which usually involved women. It was nice to have a female friend with whom one could be so comfortable. If she were to marry some local fellow, it would be bad enough, but this freakish notion of removing to London permanently, and under the auspices of that demmed popinjay Sylvester, was sheer folly.

Was he being damnably selfish? Perhaps he didn't know Roz as well as he thought he did. He had never had the slightest suspicion that she was interested in poetry. Odd she had never mentioned it. He realized, then, that it was always his interests that they discussed. He had never really bothered to get to know her. He had just taken for granted that she would always be there. Life would be different — lacking something — without her.

In Dick's carriage, a different matter was under discussion.

"You should have Lord Sylvester to dinner before he leaves, Dick," Annabelle said as they drove home. "He is so gentlemanly."

It seemed an unlikely conclusion for her to have reached, but Rosalind was pleased. "Yes, we really should," she said. "He is being so helpful to me. He is seeing about a flat for me in London."

"So odd to think of you as writing poetry," Annabelle said. "I believe I was a little hasty to dismiss Lord Sylvester from consideration as a potential suitor, Roz. The son of a marquess is bound to be well to grass. I should think you would enjoy London. So exciting compared to Croydon."

Rosalind recognized this as an effort to get her bounced out of Apple Hill, but as the ladies were of a mind, they continued to press the notion of a dinner party.

Before Miss Fortescue was dropped off at her door, it had been settled that Dick would host a dinner party the next evening. The guest list was not settled, but Rosalind was quite determined that Lady Amanda would not be invited.

What she wanted was a few guests who actually appreciated poetry and could discuss it knowledgeably with Sylvester, but as she mentally scanned her party list, she came to the sorry conclusion there was not a single poetry lover among them. It firmed her resolve to move to London.

CHAPTER
SIX

As Rosalind didn't have time to rearrange the neckline of another gown before Sylvester's call the next morning, she wore the one she had transformed for his first visit, with a different shawl to alter its appearance. The prospect of her burgeoning career, the remove to London, and Sylvester's admiration combined to act like a tonic on her spirits. A smile hovered at the corners of her lips and lit her eyes. She looked, and felt, five years younger as she fussed in front of the gilt-framed mirror in the saloon, giving her hair a final pat before his call.

Her glowing smile dimmed somewhat when she saw Lord Harwell's broad shoulders looming behind Sylvester in the saloon doorway. Sylvester smiled and came forward, while Harwell lurked behind like a shadow, frowning at her. Being in a poetical frame of mind, she was taken by the idea that Sylvester's blond radiance might stand for a symbol of goodness and light against the menace of Harwell's dark hair and swarthy coloring. She had never considered Harwell a menace before, but she sensed he was against her remove to London and might try to prevent it.

Sylvester raised her fingers to his lips. "'Full many a glorious morning have I seen' — but none has given me such pleasure as seeing you again, Miss Lovelace." Then he made a deep, playful bow.

She enjoyed the attention, but would have enjoyed it more had Sylvester come alone. She felt a little foolish with Harwell scowling in the background.

After greeting Sylvester, she said, "Harry, I didn't realize you meant to come this morning. Was there a special reason?" He often called to discuss parish or church business with her or Dick. If that was the case, she might palm him off on Dick.

"I didn't realize I needed a reason other than friendship to call," he said with a mocking grin.

"Of course not, but Lord Sylvester and I had planned to discuss my work this morning, as he has to leave soon, you know. I fear we will bore you."

"How could I be bored in such stimulating company?" he said, and walked toward the sofa.

She gave him an impatient look, then turned to Sylvester. "As it's such a fine day, I had thought we might have our discussion in the garden."

"Excellent! Perfect! It would be sacrilege to stay indoors on such a morning. 'Flowers to strew our way and bough of many a tree.'" He took her arm and she led him out to the garden, while he showered her with more floral quotations, and Harwell listened, occasionally shaking his head and rolling his eyes in amusement.

"I need not inquire who is the muse of this bower of bliss," Sylvester said, as they wandered arm in arm

58

through clouds of roses. Petals covered the ground like a carpet. Their perfume hung heavy in the air.

"I do take an interest in the roses," she admitted, blushing.

He picked one of the Provence roses that were a feature of the garden and held it to her cheek. "I see where the rose got its lovely soft petals," he said.

With Harwell's scalding eye on her, she replied woodenly, "That one is a deal pinker than my complexion, I think."

"Oh, I don't know about that, Miss Lovelace," Sylvester replied archly. "I think that pretty blush you are wearing is quite Provençal — not to be mistaken with provincial." Then he laughed at his own sort of pun.

Sylvester soon deduced it was Harwell's presence that interfered with his *à suivie* flirtation and changed the subject.

He looked all around and said, "What an inspiration this magical spot must be for you, Miss Lovelace. One wonders how you could tear your eyes away from it all to get down to the business of writing. And now — alas! — we must proceed to business as well.

"For the autumn poems, I hoped for a continuation of your theme of the cycle of life: the rich harvest of summer — paralleled, of course, with the Age of Reason — followed by the decline of human hopes and aspirations as the sun's diurnal visits shorten, plunging us into ever longer periods of darkness. This will call up a collateral memory of the Dark Ages, with the decline of learning and all cultural endeavor. We really ought to have begun with autumn — the sleep of reason, advancing to winter's symbol of the Dark Ages, on to spring's Renaissance, and so on, which you have already done so marvelously in your *Blossom Time* poems. When the oeuvre is collected into a book we shall give the seasons their proper order."

Rosalind was overwhelmed by this casual mention of her contributing four sets of poems. Why, she would be that honored figure, a regular contributor! She was particularly excited by the idea of a book. It was a heavier burden than she had anticipated. How was she to learn enough history and philosophy to tell the story of mankind through flowers in a few months? Sylvester had imagined her simple nature poems into a whole philosophy, and presumably the meaning of her falling leaves and shorter days would be similarly expounded by him in his critique.

Harwell listened with only half an ear. His greater interest was to learn what plans Sylvester had for Rosalind's remove to London. When, after a deal of poetic discussion, this topic arose, he listened closely.

"What of the flat you mentioned?" she asked Sylvester, after the *Camena* business had been settled.

"I shall discuss that with Papa when I go to Astonby. I know he has a block of flats on Glasshouse Street. I doubt they are all rented yet as he has been having them painted and repaired. They ought to be quite comfortable, and the location is good."

"What sort of rent would he charge?" she asked.

With Harwell hovering close by, Sylvester answered vaguely. "That would depend on how many rooms you

60

require. How many people will there be, besides yourself? How many servants would you be taking?"

"Only two servants, I think. A footman and a general servant who can clean and do some cooking. I shan't take a groom or carriage. I can hire a carriage when I need one. I would like to take my mount."

Harwell assumed she would also take a female companion to act as chaperon. Every atom of his body disliked the scheme, yet when he saw how happy Rosalind was, how radiant, he realized that he was being selfish. He should be happy for her. But he didn't intend to let Lord Sylvester monopolize her entirely. He was indebted to Roz for dozens of past favors.

He said, "It sounds a happy arrangement. It will do you the world of good, Roz. I shall be sure to call when I am in London and introduce you to some of my friends. You mustn't keep your nose to the grindstone night and day. You will want to socialize. Pity you haven't made your curtsy at St. James's, but there are still plenty of dos you could attend. I know your love of dancing. There are the theaters as well, concerts, exhibitions, and so on."

"Thank you, Harry," she said, surprised and pleased at his sudden volte-face.

He studied her flushed face for a moment, and she met his gaze steadily. When he spoke, his voice held a new tone of gentleness, almost regret. "It is I who should thank you for a hundred past kindnesses, which we shan't go into at the moment. I am in your debt."

Sylvester sensed a conspiratorial note creeping into the conversation. What "past favors" were these that

61

could not be discussed in front of him? Had Rosalind been Harwell's mistress? It was possible. Harwell's reputation with the ladies was pretty well known, and Miss Lovelace, living so close, must have been a strong temptation. She was no girl — must be a quarter of a century. Harwell's gaze seemed still to hold some echo of tender love as he studied her. Yes! They had been lovers. But the affair was over now, and the lady was available. An older lover would be all the crack. Lady Oxford certainly hadn't done Byron's romantic reputation any harm.

It was odd that Lord Harwell had invited him to stay at Drayton Abbey. Harwell had insisted on accompanying him this morning as well. Sylvester soon concluded that there had been an affair, it had ended without rancor, and Harwell was now trying to ease Miss Lovelace gently out of his life.

"You have only to ask if you have need of anything," Harwell was saying. "You mentioned taking your mount. You can stable it with my cattle, if you like."

Sylvester walked on a few paces, pretending to admire the flowers, but he could still hear them.

"I hadn't considered all those details," she replied. "Yes, I would like to be able to ride — but then I would need a groom."

"Rubbish, use mine. I keep a couple of fellows in London year-round for Aunt Margaret's convenience. They are sitting on their haunches most of the time."

It had been arranged that Dick would join them in the garden and invite Sylvester to dinner that evening. He was to leave them alone for an hour first, but as he was eager to get down to the orchard and see to the spraying for greenflies, he went early. Sukey accompanied him. Sandy was at her heels, making life difficult for Snow Drop. The two had not come to terms yet.

While Dick spoke to Sylvester, Rosalind said to Harwell, "Now that no big ears are eavesdropping, may I know what all this new civility is in aid of? Last night you were against my going to London. This morning you are suddenly offering bribes to be rid of me."

"Not bribes! Rewards. I have been a selfish dog, Roz. I am only trying to make your life in London as pleasant as possible and help the romance with Sylvester along."

"I don't need any help with Sylvester."

"But you do, my sweet idiot. When he said — with a great lack of originality for a poet — that your cheeks were like rose petals, you should have batted your lashes and simpered, not said in that flat voice, 'That one is a deal pinker than my complexion, I think.' That was not romantical."

"I was embarrassed. I'm not accustomed to flattery."

"Better get used to it. The new coiffure and gowns are charming." His eyes glanced off her hair and face down to admire the new neckline.

"I wish you wouldn't stare at my bosom," she said curtly, and pulled her shawl together.

"Merely admiring nature's handiwork. Breasts are the perfect example of beauty and practicality."

"Spoken like a good dairy farmer. Don't ever try to become a poet, Harry."

"I don't intend to, though it's not actually necessary for a man to be a fool to be a poet. Byron is quite sane. He gave a dandy speech in the House about the Luddite riots in Yorkshire. Pity he never followed it up with action."

"Sylvester is not a fool, nor, I hope, am I."

"I know you're not. I didn't see any mention of all that hackneyed twaddle about the Dark Ages and the Renaissance in your poems. They were just pretty verses about nature."

"Harry! You actually read them!"

"Of course I did. I felt it a duty."

She just shook her head. "How like you to not even bother pretending it was a pleasure."

"When have I ever pretended with you? Or you with me, come to that? Between us two, your Provençal roses wear their everyday name of cabbage roses."

"Only you call them that!"

"I believe in calling a spade a spade. I thought your poems were pretty. Better judges than I say they are something special. I accept their opinion and am truly happy for your success."

Once Dick had extended the invitation, he could find little to say to Sylvester. He led Sylvester over to join the other group. Sukey followed along, cradling Snow Drop in her arms to protect her from Sandy. Deprived of his amusement, Sandy gave a final bark of disgust and took off in pursuit of a squirrel.

"I have just been inviting Lord Sylvester to take his mutton with us this evening," Dick said. "I hope you will come as well, Harry."

"Thank you. I will be happy to."

"Can I come, Dick?" Sukey asked, pulling at his hand to get his attention.

"Of course not, ninnyhammer, but I'll have Cook send you up some plum cake if you manage not to rip your pinafore," Dick replied.

"I want to sit at the grown-up table!"

"When you are a little older, child," Sylvester said. "Children are to be seen, not heard."

"That's silly. What if I want something?"

"Then you ask your nanny for it."

"I told you, she's gone."

"Surely it's possible to find a replacement," he said to Rosalind. "It seems a shame to waste time when a child has so much to learn. They are peculiarly amenable to instruction at an early age, you must know. The child is not too young to begin an appreciation of good literature. I had a dozen soliloquies by heart when I was her age."

Snow Drop squirmed in Sukey's arms and succeeded in hopping down. The tassels on Lord Sylvester's top boots caught her attention, and she began leaping at them. Sylvester shook his foot to be rid of the kitten.

Sukey let out a holler. "Don't kick her! Harry, he's kicking Snow Drop!"

"Do stop your racket, Sukey!" Rosalind scolded. "And take that kitten away."

Harry picked up the kitten, tucked it into the crook of his arm, took Sukey's hand, and led her down the path toward a bench under a lilac bush. "Come along, dumbie. I'll teach you a Shakespearean sonnet. But first we'll learn the alphabet."

"I know the alphabet, Harry. Will you teach me to curse? Roz says you're good at it."

"My vocabulary is extensive to be sure, but I fear you're a little young for advanced cursing. 'Deuced' is the farthest I go with minors."

"I already know that, and 'tarnation' and 'zounds'. I learned them at the stable. 'Deuced' is not cursing."

Something twisted in Rosalind's breast when she saw Sukey and Harry, with the white kitten frolicking in his arm, walking hand in hand down the path, talking nonsense. The sun shone full on them as they left the garden. Harry's dark head was inclined down toward Sukey's tousle of curls, which shone like a golden halo. The notion of good and evil did not occur to her on this occasion.

When Sylvester began to boast how he had translated Cicero at the age of eight, she could hardly suppress a yawn. She wanted to run down the path after Harry and Sukey, and play with the kitten.

CHAPTER
SEVEN

Although the social life of Apple Hill was not dull, Rosalind was not accustomed to entertaining both morning and night. Lord Sylvester and Harwell had to be offered wine and biscuits before leaving that morning, which made the afternoon doubly busy in preparing for the dinner party. At Dick's suggestion, done to please Annabelle, it had been enlarged to include more guests and some dancing after for the younger ones. A large party, Annabelle decreed, must include Lady Amanda Vaughan. Annabelle had a great hankering after titles. Dick, thinking to help his sister, took the misguided notion of asking Annabelle over to give her a hand.

"Oh, you are planning to serve turbot and mutton again, are you?" was her comment when Rosalind outlined the main features of the menu. "I hope Lord Sylvester does not find it hopelessly rustic. I had thought you might be serving lobster and perhaps a ragout to impress him. Or oysters. Oysters would be a pleasant change."

"Cook is making her mulligatawny soup," Rosalind said apologetically. Annabelle had experience of

London cuisine and was therefore listened to with interest.

"Pity there would not be time to make a turtle soup. It is all the crack in London, but one must make arrangements for the turtle days in advance. Well, so long as you are not serving apple tart and cheese for dessert."

Here, at least, Rosalind felt she was on firm ground. "No indeed. Cook is making a Chantilly, and the gardener has some melons in the conservatory that he tells me are ripe enough to serve."

"That is a good start," Annabelle allowed. "Is there time to prepare an ice?"

"I fear not. It is only a simple dinner party, Annabelle. You know it takes an age to make ices."

"I doubt Lord Sylvester is accustomed to simple meals. We shall call it potluck. That is the excuse for country fare in London. Let me make up a centerpiece for the table. I am a bit of a dab hand at that."

Rosalind heaved a sigh of relief as she sent her troublesome helper off to the garden, armed with shears and a cutting basket. The elaborate centerpiece that was eventually placed in the center of the table hardly suggested a potluck dinner. It was quite two feet high and half again as wide. It would be impossible for the diners to see the company seated on the other side of the table. Yet it was certainly a striking arrangement, almost a miniature garden, with lilies and ferns and roses and foxglove and a bit of everything else in the garden.

"Monsieur Gervase, in London, gives lessons to ladies in flower arranging," Annabelle explained, after she had accepted praise for her handiwork. "He particularly liked my originality."

"It's lovely, Annabelle."

"And I have made up corsages for you and me, Roz. Yours is in your room. I used white roses, as I wasn't sure what gown you planned to wear. You wore your pink one last night, so I assumed it would be the green you always wore last spring."

Rosalind planned to wear the pink watered silk again, but she thanked Annabelle for the corsage.

Annabelle looked around the dining room and said, "When I take over as mistress of Apple Hill, the first thing I shall do is have this room done over. I don't know how you can stand such a gloomy place, Roz. I always feel I am eating in a pit when I take dinner here. I shall throw a bow window out, just there on the east wall, to let in the light and give a view of the gardens. When I have these dark varnished walls painted in some light color, the room will be quite nice, don't you think?"

Rosalind did not think Dick would want the wall torn apart with a bow window, but she was determined to be agreeable. "The room is certainly dark," she said. "Let us put a brace of candles on either end of the sideboard for tonight to brighten it up."

By the time the ladies went abovestairs to dress for dinner, Rosalind had a nagging headache. It was not improved to see the corsage Annabelle had left for her. It was not so much a corsage as a bouquet of roses, liberally backed by asparagus fern. When she pinned it on her gown, the weight of it pulled the material out of shape. She removed half a dozen rosebuds and pinned the corsage back in place.

Sukey came to her room before she went downstairs. "Dick says I can come down and watch the dancing for a little while," she said. This was nothing new. Sukey had been in the habit of coming down to watch the dancing for a year now without offending provincial notions of propriety. But Rosalind felt that Sylvester would dislike it, and after spending an afternoon with Annabelle, she was more determined than ever to ingratiate herself with him.

"I don't think that's a good idea, Sukey," she said. "In London, children don't go to grown-up parties. Lord Sylvester will think it uncivilized."

"I hate Lord Sylvester."

"You don't hate him. You shouldn't say such things."

"Yes, I do. He kicked Snow Drop. And he's silly. Silly Sylvester. He talks too much. I want to go watch you dance. Dick said I could."

"Well, perhaps just one dance — from the doorway. Don't be chasing about the room."

"I won't. Thanks, Roz." She hugged Rosalind, doing some damage to the corsage in the process. "I'll tell Dick you said I could come."

"Minx! You conned me!"

"Did not! Dick said I could go if you said it's all right. I'll tell him." She danced out of the room, golden curls bouncing.

Roz just shook her head. At least Sukey wouldn't be a problem in London. Dick was her legal guardian, and she would remain at Apple Hill. But she'd miss Sukey. Of course, she would visit home often. Apple Hill wasn't that far from London. And Dick would bring Sukey to visit her, too. When Sukey was older, she could make longer visits. A memory of Harry and Sukey, walking hand in hand down the garden path in the sunlight, flitted through her mind, bringing a sad smile to her lips. She would miss Harry, too. He would be at the Abbey for most of the year.

She shook the wisps of regret away and went downstairs to greet the guests. They were all old friends and neighbors. Annabelle's parents were there, along with the vicar and his wife and couples from nearby estates. Rosalind had to endure a deal of joking compliments on her first appearance in print. Her friends treated it with embarrassment, as if she had taken a tumble from her mount, or been caught tying her garter in public. Sylvester, on the other hand, was shown great respect. A lord was novelty enough, but a lord who wrote poetry and edited a magazine and wore an orange jacket (Sylvester called it bronze) was unique. Lord Sylvester, bent on acquiring subscriptions for *Camena*, was at his most charming. There wasn't a soul who escaped without promising a subscription, even Mrs Hardy, the late vicar's widow, who prided herself on never reading anything except the Bible.

The two-foot centerpiece did not prevent Lord Sylvester from talking to the table at large. His fluting voice carried above and around the mini-garden of roses, lilies, and ferns. It would be difficult to say which of his dinner companions, Lady Amanda or Miss Fortescue, was more enthralled. They both hung on his every word.

Annabelle was eager to learn more about Sylvester's family. To this end, she sat with Lady Amanda while the gentlemen took their port.

Never one to beat about the bush, she asked bluntly, "What can you tell me about Lord Sylvester's family, Lady Amanda?"

"I have known the Dunstons forever. Old Dunston, the marquess, owns half of East Sussex. Of course, his elder son, Moffat, will inherit the title and Astonby Hall, but I should think Sylvester will come into something very worthwhile. He will be a good catch for some wide-awake lady. There are no girls in the family, you must know. Sylvester, as the second son, should get his mama's dot. Twenty-five thousand, I believe it was. The estate in Surrey might very well go to him as well, from his Uncle Cyrus. Cyrus Staunton was minister of war for the Tories a few decades ago. He picked up a dozen sinecures at court."

Annabelle didn't know what a sinecure was, but as they grew at court, she felt they must be something good. "Lord Sylvester will live in London year-round, I should think," she said.

"You couldn't drive him out with a team of horses. His head is full of nothing but causing a stir with his poetry and magazine. Byron, the scoundrel, has a good deal to account for. I expect Sylvester will grow out of it, but he will never be satisfied to rusticate. He is a city creature. He lives in the family's London house. Dunston is too old to make the trip for the Season. Even Moffat seldom takes a Season, now that he is shackled."

A city creature. Annabelle was interested to learn there was a name for the cause of her particular malaise. She, too, was a city creature. She tried to like living in the country, but there was no denying she felt short-changed by having to limit herself to country assemblies and such dull dos as she had attended last night and tonight. Her own parties were much livelier, but it took more than one lady to create the sort of life she wanted.

She had tried to interest Dick in hiring a house in London for a Season after they were married, but he just said she would likely be enceinte by then, and why would she want to be rattling about London when she was in such an ungainly condition. Lord Sylvester, on the other hand, lived in a noble London mansion all year round, on close terms with the tip of the *ton*. A city creature. The phrase held the allure of sin for her.

She was the first one out the door when Dick announced that the dancing was about to begin. Only Sukey was there before her, waiting patiently on a bentwood chair against the wall. Annabelle had to have the first set with Dick, but as soon as it was over, she went to speak to Rosalind, who had been dancing with Sylvester.

"Should Sukey not be in her bed by now?" she said.

"Indeed she should. She likes to see the show — all the ladies in their finery."

She went to dispatch Sukey, who was sleepy enough that she went without an argument.

When the next set began, Sylvester, perforce, stood up with Annabelle. Their first conversation was to agree that it was foolishly lax to allow a child to attend an adults' party. That settled, Annabelle expressed a keen interest in poetry, and asked why there were none of his poems in the most recent issue of *Camena*.

"I am ashamed to say I have never read your work, milord, for I am sure you must be famous. Croydon is so backward. I had to wait two weeks to get Sir Walter Scott's *Guy Mannering*. I do miss the mental stimulation of London."

"There is nowhere like it. As Dr Johnson said, 'When a man is tired of London, he is tired of life.' Interesting you should ask why there is none of my work in the magazine, Miss Fortescue. There is nothing I like better than writing poetry, but the fact is, since I have become the editor and publisher of my magazine, I find my time pretty well filled up with the duties of running it. I have to read the submissions, you see, and decide which offerings merit publication."

"Could you not hire someone to sort out the wheat from the chaff for your final approval, and leave you free to write your marvelous poetry?"

"Now we come to the financing. I should like to hire an assistant editor eventually, but I have to keep my staff to a minimum for the present. I don't come into my inheritance for a few years. It is foolishly tied up until I am twenty-five. I am so weary of cadging from friends and relatives that I am sometimes tempted to marry a fortune." This was accompanied by a laugh to show he joked.

"I'm sure you would not have any trouble, milord," she said. "Someone of your intellectual attainments, to say nothing of your title and —" she blushed demurely and said daringly, "and your beauty."

He laughed again, but there was a different note to his voice. "Are you from a large family, Miss Fortescue?" he asked a moment later.

"No, I am the only child," she said. "If Papa had a large family to provide for, I expect he would still be in London. When a man has accumulated a good fortune and has only one to provide for, he may retire and do as he pleases — even if it does not please his daughter," the city creature added with a moue.

She saw the glint of interest in his eyes and felt she had said enough for the moment. She hoped to have another conversation with Lord Sylvester before he left, but as things turned out, Sylvester left very soon.

Lady Amanda reminded him that he was to have a look at the John Donne fragment, and as he was leaving the next day, it seemed he must go that night. He apologized profusely to Dick, then went in search of Rosalind.

"This would be such a coup for *Camena* that I mustn't hurt her feelings by refusing to go," he explained. "If she takes a huff, she might very well send the Donne fragment to *Blackwood's* or the *Edinburgh Review* in spite."

"Yes, of course you must go," Rosalind agreed. "If you get away early, you might come back for another dance. It is only ten-thirty. I expect the party will go on until one."

"That was my intention," he said with a conspiratorial smile. "You and I have not had a moment alone to get to really know one another. I feel we have more than poetry in common?" When she seemed pleased at this lure, he seized her fingers and squeezed them tightly. "I give you fair warning, Miss Lovelace, I want a deal more than words on paper from you."

She blushed like a peony and gave a breathless little laugh. Sylvester, satisfied that she was amenable to seduction, went to fetch Lady Amanda's mantle.

As Harwell watched their departure from across the room, he chewed back a smile and went to join Rosalind.

"Well, well," he said. "Now you see what you will be up against in London. The town is rife with ladies of Lady Amanda's sort. Sure you are up to it?"

"Quite sure," she replied, with a maddening smile.

CHAPTER
EIGHT

They spoke in the hallway just outside the ballroom door. "Lord Sylvester always puts the good of his magazine first, Harry," Rosalind said, with a proprietary air. "Quite rightly, too."

"I should be very much surprised if Amanda has any scribbles of John Donne's in her library," Harwell replied. "It was an excuse to snatch Sylvester out from under your nose. You may accept his departure with equanimity, but your lady guests will be heartbroken."

She gave him a tolerant smile. "He does seem to be universally pleasing, does he not? To everyone but you, I mean."

"It pleases me that he has spared me a round with Amanda. And by the by, your beau is especially pleasing to Miss Fortescue, in case you are blind and failed to notice the chit throwing herself at him."

As they spoke, Snow Drop came flying down the staircase with Sukey in hot pursuit.

"You're supposed to be in bed!" Rosalind scolded. "And you haven't even undressed yet."

"I had to go to the kitchen first to get some cake from Cook," the child replied, as if to an idiot. "I was just going to bed. I told that stupid Snow Drop to wait on my pillow, but she fell off."

Snow Drop, who considered the whole thing a game, looked over her shoulder at her pursuer, then darted into the ballroom. Sukey took off after her. Rosalind didn't see the resulting confusion, but she heard it. Some lady — it sounded like Mrs Warbuck — let out a frightened howl. There was a rather hard bump as a body hit the floor, then a moment's silence as the music wavered to a halt, followed by a buzz of voices and some laughter.

"Thank God Lord Sylvester has left!" Rosalind said, and hastened to the ballroom. Harwell gave a bah of disgust at her concern and went after her.

Mrs Warbuck, a good-natured lady, had recovered both her feet and her humor by the time Rosalind arrived. She was brushing off her skirt and straightening her turban.

"I'm so sorry. Are you hurt?" Rosalind asked.

"I'm fine. 'Twas only Sukey chasing her kitten. I didn't know what hit me at first," she said, laughing.

"I'll give her a good scold and put her straight to bed. This is really the outside of enough."

The miscreant was led forward by Dick, with Snow Drop tucked in her arms. Dick was annoyed, but Annabelle, who was with him, was livid.

"This has gone too far. The child is incorrigible!" she exclaimed. "Whoever heard of a child attending a rout party? You've got to do something with her, Dick. If you don't, I shall. I won't permit this sort of rowdiness at Apple Hill."

"It's not your house!" Sukey said.

"It soon will be!" Annabelle shot back. Her cabbage eyes narrowed into angry slits.

"I'll take her upstairs," Rosalind said, and took Sukey by the arm to lead her off. She gave her sister a good scold and warned her not to come downstairs again that night.

"I wish Dick wouldn't marry her," Sukey said, pulling her nightgown over her head. "I'm glad you'll be here to take care of me when he does. Don't stay too long in London. Come back before Dick marries her. Promise me, Roz." She directed a commanding blue gaze at her sister and hopped into bed.

"Go to sleep," Rosalind said, tucking in the blanket, but she felt like a traitor when she left the room.

This business tonight wasn't really Annabelle's fault. Sukey *was* getting out of hand. She needed firm guidance. Dick wouldn't let Annabelle abuse Sukey. There was no physical danger, but Sukey would be deuced unhappy. Rosalind determined to find a good, kind-hearted governess for her before she left for London. It was really the governess who would raise Sukey.

Rosalind still felt troubled when she returned downstairs. Harwell was waiting for her in the hall.

"I expect this will be dumped in my dish for giving her the kitten," he said.

"No, it's my fault. Sukey is getting too forward for her own good lately."

"It's not the first time she's attended one of your parties."

"It's the first time she sent one of my guests flying across the room. It really was too bad of her."

Harwell just batted his hand. "Mrs Warbuck took it in good spirit. I shouldn't worry about it."

"It's Sukey I'm worried about. I fear she and Annabelle will never rub along after I'm gone."

"Well, at least you didn't say Lord Sylvester wouldn't like it."

"No more he would," she said, with a *tsk*. "It was a good thing Amanda stole him away after all, or he would know how shabbily we go on here at Apple Hill."

"Speaking of shabby, I think he and Amanda might have waited another hour before leaving."

"Oh, he is returning," she said. "He is just going to pick up the famous fragment."

"You must root through your library and see if you have anything similar to lure him. A few lines from Spenser, a Shakespearean play scribbled on the back of a menu."

"He has already inquired whether we are related to the famous Richard Lovelace who wrote about Althea in Prison, you know. Or probably you don't know."

"I'm not a complete illiterate!" he said, offended. "I've heard of Lovelace. 'Stone walls do not a prison make, nor iron bars a cage.' Was the author some kin to you?"

"I don't think so. It seems he was from Kent, or inherited a property somewhere near here. Lord Sylvester wants to search the old family papers for a connection. I don't know when he will do it, as he plans to leave tomorrow."

"If you were wide-awake, you would invite him to spend the night. In the library, I mean!"

"I didn't think you were encouraging me to seduce him, Harry. You are not quite that bad."

"Certainly not. I never encourage older ladies to seduce minors. If you are in the mood for seduction, you must practice your charms on older gentlemen, like myself."

"If I ever feel I require practice, I shall be sure to call on you. Now, shall we stop being foolish and return to the ballroom? You haven't stood up with Annabelle. I shall hear about it if you don't."

Before they reached the ballroom, Dick came pelting out, wearing a scowl.

"Dash it, something has to be done about Sukey," he said. "Annabelle is in a pelter, calling her a hoyden and I don't know what. Can't you find her a governess, Roz? She is running wild."

"Yes, you're right. I had planned to wait until autumn, to let her have a summer free, but I see it will not do. There must be some nice girl who needs a position."

"The Rafferty girl from Croydon is at liberty," Harwell mentioned. "I was speaking to Lady Syon the other day. The chit Miss Rafferty was teaching has been sent to a ladies' academy to put the final polish on her before her presentation next spring."

"Sylvia Rafferty?" Rosalind said. "She would be perfect! Shall I speak to her, Dick, or will you? Perhaps you ought to interview her, as you are the one who will be here after I go to London."

"I wish you would forget that notion." Dick scowled. "Very well. I'll call on Miss Rafferty tomorrow. Anything to get some peace in the house."

The three returned to the ballroom. Annabelle was restored to a semblance of good humor by Harwell's company for the next set. And Harwell was chirping merrily when it was time for a midnight supper and still Lord Sylvester had not returned. Supper was an informal meal. Assorted dishes were laid out on a buffet table for the guests to fill their own plates and sit where they liked.

"It would be common of me to say, 'I told you so', " Harwell said, when he led Rosalind to the refreshment parlor, "so I shan't say it."

Rosalind was annoyed with Sylvester, but she refused to let Harwell see it. "Lord Sylvester didn't say he would be back for supper," she replied. "Merely that he would return before the party was over. He has very little interest in food, in any case."

"So I have noticed. I, on the other hand, mean to fill my plate before Dick gets all the lobster patties." Annabelle had had her way with the lobster patties. Mrs Fortescue's cook had prepared them and sent them over for the party.

They took their plates and made their selections. Rosalind sat with the Warbucks, to make more apologies for Sukey and to escape Annabelle, who sat with her parents and Dick and Harwell, very pleased to have garnered two gentlemen to her side.

Some of the older guests left immediately after supper. The younger ones stayed for a few more dances.

By one-thirty they began taking their leave, and still Sylvester had not returned. At two o'clock everyone but Harwell had left. He gave Rosalind a quizzing look.

"It seems Sylvester has got lost along the straight mile of road between here and Merton Hall," he said. "I shall keep an eye out for him on my way home. Perhaps he's wandered to the Abbey in error."

"I told him the party would be over around one. Very likely he found something interesting at Merton and stayed to examine it."

"So I assume," he murmured, repressing a smile.

"Some poetry. Very likely he stayed longer than he intended, to make a copy. I expect you will find him in bed at the Abbey when you return. Pity you stayed until the last dog was hung, only to have your little laugh at me."

He allowed his smile to blossom and stretch into a grin at her annoyance. "It was worth it," he said. "I can't remember ever seeing you so angry before, or trying so hard to conceal it. Take care you don't bust your stays."

"I do not wear stays, and I'm not in the least angry. I am happy that Sylvester found so much material for *Camena* at Merton. It will boost the circulation."

"If he disports himself in the manner approved by Amanda, he might not have to cadge off your neighbors for subscriptions the next time he calls."

"You have the mind of a sewer rat, Lord Harwell."

"Why, I only meant if he agreed to a few hands of cards with her. She likes playing cards nearly as much as she enjoys — er, other indoor sports."

"I know exactly what you meant, and if you think you are making me jealous, you are far off the mark. I am only interested in Sylvester as my editor." It was half-true at least. She was more interested in him as an editor than as a potential husband. Until she saw what other gentlemen were available in London, she would not offer Sylvester much encouragement.

Harwell just gazed at her in the shadowed ballroom, where the musicians were packing up their instruments.

"Did you know your eyelashes flutter when you're lying, Roz?" he asked.

"What makes you think I'm lying? Ladies usually flutter their eyelashes when they're flirting with a gentleman, do they not?"

He looked around the room as the musicians picked up their cases and left, each making a bobbing bow to Rosalind on the way out. They were now left alone in the room.

"You mean me? I am honored that I should occur to you as a flirt, but I must point out your coquetry is so subtle as to be unrecognized. Sewer rats seldom enter the conversation during the better class of flirtation. We ought to be extolling each other's charms."

"That would be a pretty short conversation."

"Speak for yourself! I could prose on for hours about your green eyes and fiery hair."

As his gaze lingered on these items, she felt a twinge of discomfort, until it occurred to her that Harwell was roasting her. Then she felt able to retaliate.

"You must know I prefer poetry to prose, milord. And have you not a single word of praise for my new

84

gown?" she asked, with a playful moue. "I should think when I go to the bother and expense of having a new gown made up, you might at least pretend you like it."

"It is very . . . serviceable," he said. "But I like the green muslin you hacked the top off better." She sensed a new mood creeping into the atmosphere. It was the way he said it, rather suggestively. When he reached out and took her fingers, she just looked at him, startled.

"Your turn," he said, smiling softly. "A flirtation is like weaving. The shuttle must go back and forth or the game stops. Surely a famous poetess can find something nice to say about me?"

She furrowed her brow, then said, "You're very rich, and you have a title."

"And here I thought romance was dead! Did I compliment you on your way with ciphering, or with a needle? We must soar above practicalities, my dear."

A soft smile hovered at the edges of her lips. "I did like the way you rescued Snow Drop for Sukey, when you walked in the garden with her this morning, talking nonsense about Shakespeare. That was nice, Harry."

His answering smile was gentle, more gentle than she had ever seen. "There, that didn't hurt, did it? I knew you could think of something nice to say if you really tried."

"There are lots of things about you that I like, but I shan't spoil you by praise."

"Oh, do! Spoil me!"

She hesitated a moment, thinking of Harwell's better qualities, and there were many things about him she liked. His good humor, his willing help in any time of trouble, most of all, the ease of their relationship. She said nothing, but the shadow of her thoughts lent an unaccustomed tenderness to her expression.

"You're a good neighbor," she said softly.

"That's a beginning. I was hoping for something more — personal." He looked, waiting. "Cat got your tongue? You might start with my hair. I'm not going bald, or gray."

"True, and you're not halt or lame either. I'm sorry, Harry. I can't flirt with you. I know you too well. There. This is the best I can do."

She reached up and placed a light kiss on his cheek. She had done it dozens of times, as Harwell had often kissed her in the same friendly manner. Birthdays, festive seasons, in sympathy at sad seasons, any little triumph, sometimes when he had been away and paid his first call at Apple Hill.

On those other occasions, Harwell hadn't put his arms around her waist and pulled her against him. He hadn't moved his head so that their lips brushed, sending tingles down her spine. She felt her lips quiver against his for a moment, then his arms tightened and he firmed her trembling lips with his. She gave in to the strange sensation of her first real kiss from Harwell. It was not at all as she had imagined. There was nothing rakish or dangerous in it, but only a spreading warmth and joy, followed by a strange, deep sort of yearning, like an emotional hunger.

She wanted it to go on and on. But when his hand began to move in sensuous circles over her back and he pressed her more tightly against his hard chest, she felt a treacherous flame of something she hardly recognized as passion. But she instinctively sensed the peril in it and drew away, breathless. Harry let her go without a struggle and just gazed at her in silence for a moment.

He could hardly say why he had kissed her. Roz was looking especially pretty, but then she always looked nice. Perhaps it was only the subject of their conversation — flirtation. Or perhaps it was the knowledge that she was leaving Apple Hill, moving to London. That she was romantically interested in Sylvester, whether she admitted it or not, lent her a new air of sexual interest.

She moved back a step and looked at him uncertainly, embarrassed at the unusual kiss. She smiled, expecting to see a bantering smile in return. Harwell simply went on gazing at her for a long moment, with a dark, brooding look.

"Why did you do that?" she asked.

"To see what it was like. What did you think?"

"I thought it was nice."

"Well, I daresay that's better than a slap in the face," he said in a gruff voice. Then he lifted her fingers and placed a kiss in her palm, before turning and walking away rather quickly.

She stood watching as he went toward the front hall. She felt her heart banging in her chest and a heat in her cheeks. How very strange! How had that happened, after all these years? And what would she say the next time they met? Nothing like this had ever happened between them before. She rather wished it hadn't happened now, yet she felt giddy in the aftermath of it.

CHAPTER
NINE

Rosalind felt sure Sylvester would visit her the next day before leaving Drayton Abbey. With this in mind, she arranged her toilette with care, though she didn't wear the green muslin with the adjusted neckline. She wore instead a simple gathered skirt of gamboge with a white half shirt and a green jacket, thinking the rustic style might appeal to the poet in Lord Sylvester. To match the simple outfit, she wore her hair pulled straight back from her face in a Grecian knot and donned a sunbonnet when she went out to the garden.

She wanted their last visit to be pleasant, and to avoid any altercation with Sukey, she had Dick take the child to Croydon with him for the interview with Miss Rafferty. Sylvia Rafferty was a little more than an acquaintance of the family, yet not a close friend. The ladies met regularly at church and at assemblies, but the families did not visit. Her papa had been an officer in the army. Upon his death, she and her mama had been reduced to living on his pension. When Mrs Rafferty had remarried, Sylvia had gone to work as a governess.

Rosalind was seated in the rose garden with a copy of Wordsworth's poems in her lap when she heard the crunch of boots on gravel. She decided to let Sylvester catch her unawares in this romantic setting. When the footfalls rounded the corner, she glanced up with a welcoming smile. Her smile froze. It wasn't Sylvester who had come. It was Harwell.

The memory of last night's kiss loomed up in her mind, causing some discomfort. In the bright light of day, the episode seemed like a dream. A close scrutiny of Harwell showed her no reflection of the embarrassment she was feeling. But then, what was one more kiss to Harry? He had obviously forgotten it already. Best to ignore it.

"Hullo, Harry. Where is Sylvester?" she asked, steeling herself to hear he had left without calling on her.

Harwell blinked and looked all around. "Isn't he here? He didn't return to the Abbey last night."

"What!"

Harwell lifted his eyebrows and shrugged. "It must be a disappointment to you, and when you've posed yourself so artfully in the rose garden, too. The sunbonnet is a nice touch," he added, grinning. "One assumes he found something of greater interest at Merton. Best hack another inch off your shirt, Roz. Stiff competition."

She tossed the book aside and rose angrily. "And that is why you called, to carry tales and gloat? That is odious behavior, Harry."

A scowl darkened Harwell's brow. "Of course not! I thought he was here. You mentioned last night he wished to look over some papers in the library. As he's supposed to leave for Astonby today, I assumed he had come here, worked late last night, and stayed over."

Rosalind didn't know whether she was more ashamed at Sylvester's farouche treatment, or angry with Harwell for being the bearer of the news.

"Don't shoot the messenger," he said. "And don't take a fright. He hasn't left for good. His things are still at the Abbey."

She tried to assume an easy countenance. "Naturally he wouldn't leave without saying good-bye. He is not a savage after all."

"*You* may forgive him. I think it demmed uncivil behavior not to let me know he wasn't returning last night. My butler was up till all hours, and finally went to bed with the door unlocked."

"Something must have happened to him," she cried in alarm.

He made a disparaging face. "I think we both know what 'happened' to him. Lady Amanda."

"You would think that," she scoffed. "I expect he discovered some marvelous finds in the library and fell asleep while perusing them."

"Very likely he found something marvelous, but I doubt it was in the library — and I doubt he fell asleep before investigating all the possibilities of his marvelous find."

"If you can't keep a civil tongue in your head, pray leave."

"What — leave you now, when you most need a good neighbor's shoulder to cry on?" he asked, unfazed at her outburst.

She sensed an oblique reference to their conversation of the night before and regretted her rudeness. Harry was a good neighbor. She would not let Sylvester come between her and Harry.

"You needn't look so pleased about it," she said. "Furthermore, I don't believe it for a moment. Sylvester is not like that."

"He's a man."

"Hasn't he grown up quickly? Just the other day he was a boy."

"Amanda has that effect on boys," he informed her, with a satirical grin.

She answered in the same rallying tone. "You have said what you came here to say, Harwell. If you have no more scandal to spread, you must not let me keep you from more worthwhile pursuits."

"That's not why I came! Have you ever known me to be the cause of scandal?"

"More times than I can count on the fingers of both hands."

He colored up. "Of spreading scandal, I mean."

"Oh, I can acquit you of that. You are always careful to keep your own doings under wraps, and as to the other, it takes a good deal to scandalize you — unless it involves Lord Sylvester and myself."

"Just looking out for a friend," he said. "But as my interest displeases you, I shall not interfere again. I am going to Croydon. I thought you might like me to have a word with Miss Rafferty, or deliver a note, if you prefer."

"Dick went to town to see her. Thank you anyway."

"You're welcome. Can I do anything for you while I am in town?"

"Don't forget Sukey's sugarplums," she reminded him. "You promised."

"And unlike some gentlemen, I shall keep my promise."

"Yes, eventually. Sylvester didn't promise he would return last night, you know. He merely mentioned it."

"Sylvester?" he said, feigning surprise. "How the fellow preys on your mind. I was speaking of Dick. He promised his gardener would send mine a receipt for a rose spray against black mold, but he didn't do it."

He looked, hoping to win a smile. When she didn't smile or invite him to sit down, he said good-bye and turned to leave. Before he had taken two steps, Sylvester came rushing out of the house into the garden.

"I am covered in shame!" he cried, first to Harwell, then to Rosalind. "What must you think of me? Such untoward behavior. Really I cannot find words to say, except I am extremely sorry."

A glance showed he had not met with any physical violence. His clothing was intact, his face unmarked. "What happened, milord?" she asked.

"You'll never guess who was at Merton when we arrived!"

"Byron?" Rosalind exclaimed.

"Byron? No, I would hardly stay away all night for Lord Byron," he scoffed. "He was run out of Town a year ago in any case. No, it was Coleridge. He landed in at midnight. It turns out he was a great friend of Lady Amanda's mama."

Roz was coming to realize Sylvester was intensely jealous of any young poet who was well known. Coleridge was old enough to have become a legend, and was therefore above reproach.

She sighed. "How I should love to have met him!"

"You shall, Miss Lovelace."

"Is he coming here?"

"Alas, he had to leave early this morning, which is why we were up half the night talking. Well, he did most of the talking, while I listened at his feet."

"That was a change," Harwell murmured. Rosalind glared at him, but Sylvester took the comment in good spirit.

"Ah, you are being satirical, Harwell," Sylvester said, laughing. "It is true, one cannot get a word in edgewise when Coleridge is in the room, but then, his conversation is always so enlightening that one is content to sit and listen, and learn. He has agreed to write an essay for the next issue of *Camena*."

"I see you did manage to get a few words in," Harwell said.

Sylvester, still reeling with triumph, said, "Oh, certainly. I always take every opportunity to advance my cause."

"When can I meet him?" Rosalind asked eagerly.

"As soon as we get you installed in Glasshouse Street. He is most eager to meet you. He feels certain Wordsworth will also want to make your acquaintance."

Rosalind was pleased that Sylvester had a good excuse for having remained away overnight and thrilled at the prospect of rubbing shoulders with these poetic giants.

"What of the John Donne fragment?" Harwell asked. "Will it do for *Camena*?"

Lord Sylvester rolled his eyes. "The rhyme was by a Joan Dunne. Honestly, I ask you! Lady Amanda has no notion of poetry. 'Twas mere doggerel."

Harwell murmured that he was sorry. He noticed that, while Sylvester had left Apple Hill at ten-thirty for a one-mile drive to Merton, he had still been there at midnight when Coleridge arrived. Had it taken him over an hour to discover the few lines were mere doggerel?

"I'm afraid I must be dashing off," Sylvester said a moment later. "I shall pay only a fleeting visit to Papa, and stop by again on my way to London to let you know about the flat on Glasshouse Street, Miss Lovelace. I shall be back in five days' time."

He thanked Rosalind a few times, thanked Harwell for his hospitality, said his farewells, and took his departure. Harwell continued on to Croydon. Rosalind remained alone in the garden. Beneath all her joy and triumph, she was aware of a troubling shadow. She had been a little hard on Harry. Perhaps he hadn't come to gloat after all. Sylvester should have let him know he would not be returning last night. He should have let her know as well. Still, Sylvester was young, and one did not get many opportunities to spend an evening alone with the great Coleridge. And soon she would meet him.

CHAPTER
TEN

Dick returned a little later with good news. Sukey and Miss Rafferty had gotten along famously. And Miss Rafferty had agreed to assume the position of governess. Indeed, she was so eager for the post that she would come to begin work the very next day.

"Annabelle will be happy to hear it," Rosalind said. And she was happy, too. Sylvia Rafferty was exactly the sort of lady she had hoped to find. She had been well educated, she would be sensible and firm, yet was young and pleasant enough that she wouldn't frighten Sukey to death.

Dick received a note from Annabelle that morning inviting Rosalind and him to take potluck dinner at her house that evening. It was not a party, just a family dinner, and therefore required no elaborate toilette.

The minute they were inside her door, her first conversation was about Lord Sylvester. She was unhappy to hear that he had left, but her temper improved when she learned he would be returning in five days.

"I shall have a little rout party that evening," she announced.

"I'm not sure he will be remaining overnight," Rosalind said, although she intended to invite him to do so.

"Oh, you must invite him!" Annabelle said at once. "He will be quite fagged after coming all the way from Astonby."

"Is it far away?" Rosalind asked. Sylvester had not given her any details of his ancestral home.

"Yes, quite sixty miles away. I looked him — it up in *Debrett's Peerage*. If he leaves in the morning, he will be too fagged to continue on to London that same night, so I shall have a dinner party and rout after. We don't want him to think we are complete bumpkins."

This slur on the entertainment provided for his lordship thus far passed without comment, but not without being noticed.

"That is very kind of you," Rosalind said. She was grateful that she would not be put to the nuisance of entertaining Sylvester again.

"Papa suggested we should invite him to stay here with us overnight. You don't mind, Roz?"

"An excellent notion!" Dick declared at once.

Rosalind offered no objection. In fact, she was aware of a feeling of relief. There was no denying Sylvester in large doses could be fatiguing. She felt it was not Sylvester himself so much. It was just that Dick, Sukey, and Harwell did not care for him. Once she was away from them in London, she would be able to enjoy Sylvester's company without worrying.

"You will be happy to hear I have found a governess for Sukey," Dick said. "Miss Rafferty, right here in Croydon, has agreed to come to us."

"Miss Rafferty?" Annabelle said, frowning. "I'm not sure she is the woman I would have chosen. She is a little common."

"Common? Why, she has spent the last few years taking care of Lady Syon's girl. She is up to all the rigs."

"You ought to have consulted me first, Dick. I had in mind someone older." Miss Rafferty was a deal too pretty to be welcome under Annabelle's roof.

"Since we were in a bit of a hurry . . ." Dick said.

"Of course. She will do until we find a good ladies' academy for Sukey. It will be only for a year or so."

Dick had found that the best way to go on with his beloved was to proceed one step at a time. He had no notion of sending Sukey off to an academy, but he would fight that battle when the time came.

Next morning he sent his rig off to Croydon for Miss Rafferty. He was very well pleased with her. She was a sensible girl who thought much as he and Rosalind did on the subject of raising youngsters. During the summer the lessons were confined to the mornings. In this fine weather the afternoons were more likely to be spent in walks and rides and an occasional drive in the afternoon. The long, cold winter would be time enough to get down to serious work. She drove Sukey into Croydon one day in the donkey cart to visit her mama, now Mrs Simpson, the wife of a retired merchant.

It was eventually borne in on Dick that Miss Rafferty was dashed pretty. Not an out-and-outer like Annabelle, certainly no fine airs and graces about her, but she had a friendly, open face, warm brown eyes, and a wide smile.

The next few days passed with no major catastrophe. Annabelle called each day at Apple Hill to discuss plans for her rout party with Rosalind. It was clear that it was to be the grandest do ever held in Croydon. Half a dozen musicians had been hired, a new gown made up in a hurry, a new coiffure arranged, and a pastry chef imported from London for the occasion.

Annabelle made a point of speaking to Miss Rafferty each time she was at Apple Hill. On her last visit, the day before Sylvester's return, she found a complaint.

"You were seen in Croydon yesterday, Miss Rafferty," she said, in an accusing way.

"Yes, ma'am. I look Sukey to visit my mama."

"I'm not sure that was wise. You are paid to teach Miss Susan, not entertain yourself."

"My mama was feeling poorly. I felt I ought to visit her, and since she is so close . . ."

"There is nothing amiss in that," Dick said at once. "Miss Rafferty asked my permission before going."

"Lady Syon never objected when I took her daughter to call on Mama," Miss Rafferty said.

"We are not Lady Syon!" Annabelle said angrily.

"Of course not, Miss Fortescue," Miss Rafferty said, rather ambiguously.

If Lady Syon permitted such visits, then Annabelle assumed it was a solecism for her to have objected. To give herself an excuse, she said, "I hope your mama is not suffering from anything contagious?"

"Oh no, Miss Fortescue. It was the toothache."

Stymied on all counts, Annabelle turned her ire on Dick. "If your sister is to be driven into town, Dick, you ought to have given her the use of the carriage. What will everyone think to see your sister in a donkey cart?"

"Why, if they cared, or had any common sense, they would think I was using the carriage that day myself, as I was."

Annabelle's cheeks turned pink. "You may leave us now, Miss Rafferty," she said.

Miss Rafferty was glad to escape. She felt free enough with her employer by this time to make a little grimacing, apologetic face behind Miss Fortescue's back before darting out the door. Dick smiled and winked. As soon as she was gone, Annabelle turned her wrath on him.

"How dare you take her side against me! And in front of her, too. We must stick together or the servants will walk all over us. Really, I am very dissatisfied with Miss Rafferty. She is an uncommonly sly, encroaching creature. I shall look about for someone more responsible to replace her."

"We are happy with Miss Rafferty," Dick said as Rosalind joined them.

"Well, I am not! Every time I call, she is out playing with Sukey. When does she teach the child anything?"

"They spend the morning in the schoolroom. The weather is so fine just now . . ." Rosalind said placatingly.

"And taking her to visit that mother! I doubt very much that Lady Syon permitted anything of the sort. Do you know who the mother is married to? A merchant!"

"What is wrong with that?" Dick asked at once. "Her papa was an officer and a gentleman. In fact, he was a dashed hero in the Peninsula."

"It won't do," Annabelle said firmly. Then she proceeded to the conservatory to tell the gardener what bouquets he should send for her rout party.

In the saloon, Rosalind turned a troubled face to Dick. "I do hope she doesn't turn Miss Rafferty off. I think we were very fortunate to get her."

"She'll not turn her off. I am still the master here, and I am very well satisfied with Syl— Miss Rafferty." On this firm speech, Dick rose and strode angrily to his study.

Rosalind felt a stab of apprehension. Perhaps Dick was becoming too fond of Miss Rafferty. Rosalind hadn't noticed it, but no doubt a fiancée was more attuned to such things. Perhaps Annabelle had seen that wink as Miss Rafferty left. She must warn Dick to be more discreet.

It was odd, too, that Dick had no objection to Lord Sylvester staying with the Fortescues when Annabelle was quite obviously infatuated with him — or his title. Rosalind herself had no worry on that score. Lord Sylvester would have nothing in common with Annabelle. She feared he would not find any of the Fortescues congenial, but it was only for one night.

CHAPTER
ELEVEN

Annabelle was once again at Apple Hill when Lord Sylvester returned in five days' time, as promised. In fact, she had been there since half past one, and he did not arrive until four. She was extremely eager to get home and keep an eye on the party preparations, almost as eager as her hostess was to be rid of her.

Rosalind noticed at once that Sylvester's exultation at having met Coleridge had worn off. He wore a petulant face when he stepped into the saloon. It struck her that he looked like a sulky little boy, closer to twelve than twenty-two. There was no deluge of poetic quotations expressing his pleasure at seeing her again.

"Good day, Miss Lovelace," he said, and made one of his exquisite bows.

"How was your visit to Astonby?" she asked, when he had spoken to Annabelle and was seated in the saloon.

"Not so fruitful as I had hoped," he replied curtly. "Papa refused to advance me any of my money to run *Camena*. My own money, mind you! Oh, don't worry that I shall have to close down entirely. Lady Amanda has expressed some interest, though I am not sure it would be wise to accept anything from her. And of course, the subscriptions are picking up every day. We shall pull through, but I had hoped to enlarge the magazine and upgrade the quality of the presentation and articles. You have to pay the established writers a decent price to contribute something. And of course, there is advertising. One cannot rely entirely on word of mouth. The advertising does not come cheap."

"All that takes a little time," Rosalind said supportively.

"Indeed it does, and a deal of work. At least it is all arranged about your flat. Papa says the painters have left, so you can move in anytime it suits you. You will want to see about furnishings and so on." He mentioned a rent that was not only reasonable but a bargain.

Annabelle sat listening, with every fiber of her being wishing that flat in London were to be hers. That she were the one to share Sylvester's troubles, two city creatures, struggling together.

"And now I must be getting on," he said, rising. "I shall be in London by nightfall if I get away early. I am sorry to dash off so quickly, Miss Lovelace, but soon we will be together for long visits."

Until this point, Annabelle had been sitting, quietly listening. At this speech, she was suddenly thrown into a tizzy.

"Oh, Lord Sylvester, you cannot leave today! I have planned a dinner especially in your honor!"

Sylvester received this news with considerable astonishment, and very little pleasure. In fact, with an air of pique. How should she have planned a party for him when they were virtual strangers, and to do it without even making sure he would be here at the time?

"I'm sorry if it inconveniences you, Miss —" What was the chit's name? "Miss Montague."

"Fortescue," she said. "I am engaged to Miss Lovelace's brother, you recall. Oh, but you must stay! I have promised all my friends they would meet you this evening. They are looking forward to it so. And Papa! He wants to hear all about the *Camena*."

He recalled, then, that her papa was a wealthy man. He might very well invest in the magazine, when his son-in-law's sister was gaining fame through it. These rich cits liked to rub elbows with the *ton*. A largish party would yield many subscriptions to *Camena*. And of course, it was always flattering to be told people were eager to meet him.

"I have a great many calls I must make in London," he said, but he said it in the tone of a man who might be dissuaded from the path of duty.

"Just one night," Annabelle said, adopting a moue that always worked with Dick.

"Well, perhaps one night. Truth to tell, I am fagged. I shall put up at a hotel and —"

"You must stay with us, Lord Sylvester," Annabelle said at once.

Sylvester cocked an assessing eye at Rosalind. "You are perfectly welcome to stay here," she said, rather dutifully. Sylvester swiftly conned his options. But under Rosalind's own roof, and with her brother here as well, nothing could come of their affair.

Annabelle's greater enthusiasm carried the day. "You will be closer to London if you stay overnight in town," she said. "And we have a dozen empty rooms. Mama is so eager to become better acquainted with you."

With this and other blandishments, and no very strenuous objection from Rosalind, it was settled. Sylvester followed Annabelle's spanking new landau into Croydon, to a magnificent mansion whose fine old Tudor lines were rapidly being blurred by the throwing out of bow windows and the replacement of leaded glass by large, clear panes that gave a sharper view of the High Street.

Rosalind's only worry was that Lord Sylvester would find the Fortescues overweeningly encroaching, and that the Fortescues would find Sylvester toplofty. Even these concerns dwindled as she made her toilette for the party. The evening was cool enough for her to wear her autumn evening gown of russet silk with the open skirt in front showing a gold taffeta underskirt. With the upstairs maid's contrivance (she had never bothered to hire a dresser), she achieved a coiffure worthy of the gown. It was a nest of curls copied from *The Ladies' Magazine*.

When she met Dick in the saloon, he said, "Where is Miss Rafferty?"

"Miss Rafferty is not invited, Dick," Rosalind replied.

"Ah, she is only coming to the rout party after dinner, then. I shall send the carriage back for her."

"She is not coming at all."

Dick's brow darkened. "Why not? Sylvia is always invited to Annabelle's large parties. I have met her at them a dozen times."

"Now that she is working for you, I expect Annabelle wishes to keep the relationship on a more businesslike footing."

"Dash it, her working for us is all the more reason to invite her. She is a lady after all, her papa was a major. Why, she can speak French."

"Well, it is too late now. You can speak to Annabelle, and another time —"

"I shall have a word with Sylvia before we leave. I daresay she is blue-deviled at missing out on the party. I think it very petty of Annabelle to take this attitude. As if it weren't bad enough, her having this lavish do for Sylvester, whom she scarcely knows, but to go leaving Sylvia out on purpose!"

As he finished, Sukey came pelting down the front stairs, with Miss Rafferty rushing behind her. Miss Rafferty displayed not the least trace of being blue-deviled. She wore her usual smile.

"Miss Sukey pestered me into letting her see you both all dressed for the party. I hope I have not done wrong to let her come down to say good night."

"I always come to see how Roz looks," Sukey told her. "Oh, you're wearing that again," she said, shaking her curls at Rosalind's autumn gown. "What did you do to your hair? It looks funny."

"You look very nice, Miss Lovelace," Miss Rafferty said. Then she shyly turned to examine Dick.

"Well, don't I look nice, too, Miss Rafferty?" he asked, striking a pose.

"Very nice, Mr Lovelace," she replied.

Rosalind felt a recurrence of those vague stirrings of apprehension. There was a certain tension in the air. Dick was preening like a gentleman after a lady, though Miss Rafferty behaved very properly.

Dick had called Miss Rafferty "Sylvia" a moment ago. Now he called her Miss Rafferty. Which was his usual way of addressing her? Was that "Miss Rafferty" said to lend a businesslike air to what had become more than business between them? Or had the "Sylvia" betrayed the way he thought of her in his secret heart? Either way, it did not bode well for his coming marriage.

"Come and kiss us good-bye, Sukey," Rosalind said. Sukey threw her arms around her sister, dislodging her shawl in the process, then hopped into Dick's arms for a whirl that nearly knocked over the vase of flowers on the table.

"Oh, Mr Lovelace, do be careful!" Miss Rafferty exclaimed, and rescued the tumbling vase.

Rosalind, listening, thought that "Mr Lovelace" would have been "Dick" if the two were on a more familiar footing. In her excitement, she would have used the first name that came to mind.

When Dick put Sukey down, he looked at Miss Rafferty with a self-conscious smile.

"I'm sorry you aren't coming with us, Miss Rafferty," he said.

"Have a dance for me. And some of Miss Fortescue's lobster patties," she replied. If she was heartbroken to be left at home, she didn't reveal it by so much as a blink as she took Sukey's hand and led her back upstairs.

"Next time I shall insist that Annabelle invite Miss Rafferty," was all Dick said about it, but he said it in a very determined voice.

Several carriages were on the road as they headed toward Croydon. Rosalind recognized two or three of them as belonging to friends who would be at the party. Harwell, who always drove like a madman, shot past them in his curricle and waved from the perch.

He was waiting for them outside Fortescue's mansion when they alit. As his dark eyes raked Rosalind, she observed that he was wearing a new jacket. Its cut told her it was from Weston, London's premier tailor. The dark bottle green looked well against his swarthy face, with the flash of an immaculate cravat adding a contrast. His cravat pin was an emerald so dark it looked black.

"Yes, it is last year's gown," she said.

"But this year's coiffure. *Très chic*, Miss Lovelace. I am happy to see that modest gown. I feared Miss Fortescue's nobbling of Sylvester might have led you to some immodest excess with your shears. Or did you give her arm a tweak to talk her into this party?"

"It was Annabelle's idea."

"A pity the guest of honor won't be here," he said.

"What?"

"Don't be alarmed. He's not injured. He stopped at the Abbey on his way from Astonby. He planned to go straight through to London this evening. Pity, after your careful toilette."

She let him gloat a moment, then said, "Not straight through, Harry. He stopped at Apple Hill to see us. We convinced him to remain for the party. In fact, he will be staying overnight."

Harwell's lips pinched into a thin line. He betrayed only an instant's annoyance before smiling. "That'll teach me to count my chickens before they're hatched."

"Why were you so eager to hatch that particular chicken, I wonder?"

"Selfishness, pure and simple. I dislike the notion of losing you. To London, I mean."

"I, on the other hand, always look forward to your taking off for London," she retorted.

"It's the sugarplums that accompany me back that you look forward to, no doubt."

"What sugarplums? Sukey is still waiting."

"Good Lord! Didn't I give her any?"

"What a convenient memory you have."

As he took her arm and led her to the door, he said, "I shall buy them the next time I am in Croydon."

"Promises, promises."

CHAPTER
TWELVE

The party was a fiasco or a wild success, depending on one's point of view. The food was good and plentiful to the point of excess. Wine of the most expensive sorts flowed freely from the moment Rosalind entered the lavish saloon, whose more garish excesses in the way of red brocade and gilt were hidden behind bushels of flowers.

Twenty-four sat down to a dinner that would have satisfied a glutton, but perhaps not the refined taste of a Lucullus. Still, one did not have to eat soup and turbot and lobsters and oysters. Ham, mutton, three kinds of fowl, roast beef, pork, and rabbit need not all be tried. There was certainly something for every taste, and a host of desserts of all kinds, from a simple syllabub to a cake in the shape of a magazine, with *Camena* inscribed in gold and colored icing on its surface. A wedge of simple apple tart with cheddar was smuggled to the board as well for Mr Fortescue.

Anyone but a cannibal could find a meal to his liking amid the bewildering array of choices. Even Lord Sylvester was tempted to stop talking for a few moments and eat a stalk of asparagus and an oyster.

When it was over, the ladies staggered to the saloon to sit benumbed until the gentlemen joined them. Half an hour was not really sufficient time to digest such a gargantuan repast, but the moment the gentlemen appeared, Annabelle ushered them to the ballroom, where more delights awaited their jaded eyes. The other guests who had been invited to only the rout began to arrive to swell their numbers.

It was difficult to credit that Annabelle had transformed the ballroom into a Persian tent in only five days, but she had done it, and spiced the room up with an overpowering aroma of incense as well. Pleated muslin covered the ceiling and half the walls. The baroque chandeliers peeked through the muslin, casting refracted light on the stalls of flowers and fruit and vegetables placed between the chairs at the sides of the room. The musicians were dressed in Persian costumes hired from London for the occasion.

"I wager Lord Sylvester has not seen anything to beat this in London," Annabelle said, as she stood with Dick and Rosalind at the doorway, admiring her handiwork while waiting for the music to begin.

"You've gone to a deal of trouble for a fellow you hardly know." Dick scowled. He was not thinking of his own much simpler birthday party as Annabelle thought, but of how Sylvia would have loved to see this extravaganza.

"It's not just for him," she replied. "I wanted to show you how well I can entertain, too. I would like to have a do like this for our wedding party, Dick."

"Dash it, we ain't Persians. Next you will be saying you want to go to Paris for the treacle moon."

"Oh no! Italy, I think. Lord Sylvester was telling me that everyone should see Rome before he dies. Or was it Greece? One of those foreign places anyhow. Not Paree. That's how the French pronounce it."

Lord Sylvester had the first dance with Rosalind. He had not come prepared for such a gala affair and wore again the same canary yellow jacket he had worn to Harwell's small party.

"This do must have set Fortescue back a small fortune," he said, looking around assessingly. "Such excess is in wretched taste, of course. Had Miss Fortescue consulted me as to what sort of party I would like, I could have spared her the tent and three-quarters of the menu. I would rather have had the blunt put into *Camena*."

"Don't feel guilty at the expense. I expect the party was as much to display Miss Fortescue's talents as for you. She is from London, you know, and finds our dos hopelessly provincial."

"Yes, she was mentioning that she misses London dreadfully. You ought to have her to Town for a visit, Miss Lovelace. I think her papa might do something handsome for *Camena* if we showed her about a little."

The irony of inviting Annabelle to London, when the major reason for going was to escape her, was not wasted on Rosalind.

"She will be busy with her wedding plans," she said.

"Still, she seemed mighty interested in going to London. It is all she speaks of."

Rosalind didn't encourage this notion. The surest way of diverting Sylvester's attention was to let him prattle on about his magazine. She broached the subject, then looked about to see who Harwell was dancing with while Sylvester answered at some length. She saw that Lady Amanda, wearing a strident yellow-and-black-striped gown and gold turban and looking like a gigantic bumblebee, had captured Harwell and was bouncing him about the square.

When the set was over, Harwell joined Rosalind and Sylvester.

"Lady Amanda has been wanting to speak to you," he said to Sylvester.

"Naughty boy!" Lady Amanda said, as she got a grip on Sylvester's elbow and led her captive away.

"Well," Harwell said to Rosalind, "Miss Fortescue has certainly put us all in the shade with this do. Take care or she'll be snapping Sylvester out from under your nose. This wild extravagance is all in his honor, n'est-ce pas?"

"I believe he is just the pretext to show us what she can do when she puts her mind to it."

"Her mind and her papa's lucre. This must have set him back a packet. Shall we go to the refreshment tent to escape that sickening smell? What the devil is it?"

"Incense, Harry."

"Ah, incense for the great god Sylvester. He certainly knows how to impress the ladies."

"Yes, it is quite a novelty for a gent to go out of his way to impress us with cultured conversation, or

112

anything but setdowns and condescension. We provincials never open a book."

"I didn't mean you!" he said, then flushed as he realized that this was exactly what he had meant.

They strolled out of the ballroom, arguing amicably. The refreshment parlor felt cool and fresh after the bazaar-like atmosphere of the crowded ballroom.

"Champagne!" he exclaimed, when he glanced at the refreshment table. "Is Sylvester suitably appreciative of all this, I wonder?" he asked, handing her a glass.

"He regrets that the money wasn't spent elsewhere. I think you know where."

He peered over his glass at her. "Do I detect an irreverent note of cynicism creeping in?" he asked archly.

"No, a note of common sense."

A smile quirked Harwell's lips. "That is music to my ears!"

"I mean I agree with him. His papa wouldn't forward him any money."

"Dunston is no fool."

"You think it foolish to foster culture, Harry? How very like you!"

"I think it foolish for a youngster to squander his patrimony on a magazine that is doomed to failure. These literary rags seldom make a go of it."

"I see it as a beautiful, idealistic quest."

"Yes, the sort that ruins a man."

"Or makes his reputation. Who would have heard of Leigh Hunt if it were not for his *Examiner*?"

"I hope this doesn't mean you're thinking of putting your dowry into *Camena*."

She was shocked at the idea. "Of course not! I can't afford it."

"Then you assume financial disaster for Sylvester's venture. I think I have just made my point. Why are you really running off to London, Roz?"

"To broaden my literary and artistic horizons," she said vaguely. He scoffed. "What's the matter, Harry? You don't want me there, seeing how scandalously you behave when you're away from the Abbey? Don't worry. I shan't be seeing you much, and I shan't carry tales back home." She added rather smugly, "I shall be too busy having my own life, for a change."

"You have a good life here. And what of Sukey? I hear Miss Fortescue is not happy with Miss Rafferty, though I think her a very good sort of girl myself."

"Where did you hear that?"

"In town," he said with a shrug. Obviously Annabelle had been spreading word of her unhappiness with Miss Rafferty.

"Annabelle thinks Sukey ought to be sent to an academy in a few years," Rosalind explained. "And don't bother frowning at me! Dick is her guardian, and he is under Annabelle's paw. Annabelle doesn't want me in the house. She's quite right. If I stayed, we would only come to cuffs. I'm just a busybody old spinster, as you said."

"I didn't say that!"

"You said something very like it the other day."

"I didn't say busybody."

"It was the 'old spinster' that stung."

"I was only funning!"

She gave a dismissing *tsk*, as if not believing him, or caring much what he thought. A frown grew between his eyebrows.

"Roz, you do realize that Sylvester runs with a pretty racy set in London? I have been making a few inquiries . . ." He hesitated, wondering how much he should say. It was only rumors, after all.

She gave him a cold stare. "How . . . considerate of you."

"It was your own idea. You said I oughtn't to hand you over to just any old hedge bird."

"Odd, I seem to recall your saying quite recently that Sylvester is too young and innocent for me."

"You have a way of hearing what you want to hear. I did not say too innocent, just too young."

She took a sip of her champagne before answering, in a pensive mood, "It's time I shed my innocence."

Harwell's frown deepened to a dark scowl. "Rosalind, listen to yourself! What's happened to you? You were always the sensible one."

"Did it ever occur to you I might be tired of being the sensible one? I'm four and twenty years old, Harry, and I've never had a life. That's what has happened to me. I run the house and do the bookkeeping for Dick. I look after Sukey. I run errands for you when you're away, and help clean up the shambles you've made of your love affairs. I know more about the parish than the vicar."

His scowl dwindled to a troubled gaze as he considered what she had said and admitted that she had a point. But surely Sylvester Staunton was not the answer to her problem. "You have your poetry," he said. It still seemed odd to him that sensible Roz was a closet poet. How little he really knew about her. From her pleasant manner, he had always assumed she was happy with her lot.

"Scribbling alone in bed at night to keep the blue devils at bay is a poor substitute for a life. I want more than that."

"But your excuse — *reason* for going to London is to involve yourself more in the poetry."

She gave a dismissing gesture with her hand. "I want to do things, meet people."

"People are people all over the world. They're not that different in London."

Her chin rose, and she said challengingly, "Perhaps I want to find a husband. There, I've said it."

He leapt on it like a cat on a mouse. "So you *are* chasing after Sylvester!"

She refused to backtrack. "He wants me to go. We shall see if anything comes of it. We've only known each other a few days. I find him interesting — a pleasant change from gentlemen who think of nothing but farming."

"I think you're making a big mistake. I wish you would stay at Grosvenor Square, for a while, at least. Some of the tenants in that place on Glasshouse Street are no better than they should be. Failed artists and actors and such."

"And minor poets?" she asked, arching an angry eyebrow at him. "I'm not interested in making my curtsy at St James's, Harry. I am going for personal fulfillment."

"You mentioned finding a husband . . ."

"How else does a lady fulfill herself? Poetry is fine, but it's only a substitute for life. I think we have plucked this poor crow to death. Let us return to the bazaar."

A reluctant smile peeped out. "At least you didn't say 'the party'. You're not enjoying this do any more than I am."

"I was enjoying it — until you came with your thunderclouds to spoil it."

Of course, it wasn't the party that Harwell had spoiled. Roz found it quite as ridiculous and enjoyable as any sane person would. It was her going to London that he was spoiling with all his carping. Why shouldn't she go? Why shouldn't she have a life, like everyone else? She had done her share and more for the family and Apple Hill. She had already lost one fiancé to it. How much more did she owe? The house and the greater part of the family fortune had been left to Dick. It was for him to make suitable arrangements for Sukey. Her head began to ache with the worry of it all.

After a few more sets, her headache worsened and she told Dick she would go home and send the carriage back for him.

"I'll go with you," he said at once. "I've had enough of this do."

"Won't Annabelle be offended if you leave?"

"She'll never miss me. She is too busy preening herself over this ridiculous festival."

They went to thank the Fortescues for the party. Sylvester and Annabelle were with them, standing at the door of the ballroom.

"You've heard the wonderful news?" Annabelle said, smiling at Dick. "Papa is going to invest a little something in Lord Sylvester's magazine. Lord Sylvester will come back to discuss it in a few days, after he has taken care of some important business in London."

Dick scowled and said, "Congratulations, milord. I'm taking Roz home, Belle. She has the megrims."

"That is good news," Rosalind said to Sylvester. She wondered how the hard-headed Fortescue had been cajoled into parting with his blunt and how much he had invested. Remembering Harry's warning, she hoped it was not a very large sum. Fortescue would do anything to please Annabelle. One had only to look into the ballroom to see how his daughter bear-led him.

Sylvester walked Rosalind to the door. "I'm so happy for you, Lord Sylvester!" she said in a low voice.

"Dash it, isn't it time you stopped lording me? Call me Sylvester, Rosalind."

"Very well, if you like. How did you manage it?"

He drew her aside and spoke in a whisper, while Dick took his leave of Annabelle and her parents.

"I mentioned Miss Fortescue's visiting you in London. Don't worry about it. I shall give you the larger flat with an extra bedchamber."

"I'm not sure I can afford it."

He looked down at her and gave an intimate laugh. "Don't worry about the expense. I will take care of all that. We shall have to entertain her a little, but we will still find plenty of time to be alone. I'll call on you the minute I get back. Will you miss me as much as I miss you?"

She said in confusion, "Oh, indeed."

As she and Dick drove home Rosalind wondered at Sylvester's secretive manner, his whispering in her ear. When he said not to worry about the extra expense, he would take care of it all, she assumed he meant he would give the larger flat at the price of the smaller. But that implied that Annabelle would be spending a long period of time with her. Surely she didn't plan to move in for anything like a month, so close to her wedding? Of course, she had often spoken of buying her trousseau in London, so perhaps that was why she wished to go. Annabelle was a famous shopper. Finding time alone with Sylvester would be no problem.

That mention of time alone gave her some satisfaction. Not just time away from Annabelle, but time alone. Only courting couples worried about that. Sylvester was coming to care for her. She felt a bubble of triumph, but not the deep joy she would feel if she knew she cared for him. Did she care for him in that way? She had not been alone with him enough to find out, but in London she would be.

When she turned an ear to Dick's grumbling, he was saying, "I don't see why she couldn't have invited Miss Rafferty to the rout at least. She had the Gibbons's governess there, and that Miss Milchamp who does sewing for ladies. Dash it, Miss Rafferty would have loved the party. If Annabelle thinks I am getting married in a tent, she has another think coming, I can tell you."

"I'm sure that's not what she meant. She only means she wants a large do."

"I've a good mind to elope," he said mutinously.

CHAPTER
THIRTEEN

Rosalind spent the next morning sorting through her clothes-press to select the gowns she would take to London and making a list of small purchases to be made before she left. That afternoon she drove into town to begin looking for the silk stockings and other items on her list. Miss Rafferty asked her if she would mind buying a present for Sukey while she was in town.

"I didn't realize her birthday is tomorrow until she mentioned it, Miss Lovelace, or I would have made her something."

"You don't have to buy her anything," Rosalind said.

"Oh, but for her birthday! Just a small present. They have children's games and books at the everything shop. What do you think she'd like?"

"Why don't you and Sukey come along with me?" Rosalind suggested. "You can let Sukey choose for herself while I'm in the drapery shop."

Miss Rafferty's eyes lit with pleasure, then dimmed. "I wouldn't want her to know what the present is before tomorrow. I could take her to the shop and discover what strikes her fancy, then take her to meet you, and slip back and buy it. Would you mind looking after her for a few minutes?"

"Not at all. I'll keep Sukey in the drapery shop and let her choose some ribbons to keep her busy."

"When I leave the toy shop empty-handed, she'll think I'm not buying whatever it is she's chosen," Miss Rafferty said with an air of intrigue. "I do want to surprise her."

Rosalind had nearly forgotten the keen enthusiasm of youth. With so many real responsibilities on her shoulders, such simple pleasures as secret gifts had become a thing of the past. Miss Rafferty's eagerness reminded her of past birthdays when she used to hide Dick's present, and he enjoyed searching for it almost as much as the gift itself.

"Cook's making her up a grand cake with white and pink icing," Miss Rafferty continued. "I thought we might have it in the garden, a sort of tea party, if the weather allows. Would it be all right?"

"That's a lovely idea!"

Rosalind liked, too, that Miss Rafferty had asked her, and not gone begging favors of Dick. It proved to her satisfaction that she and Dick had not been carrying on in secret.

"What are you giving her, Miss Lovelace, if you don't mind my asking?"

"The doll she's been hinting for since Christmas."

"The one in Marshall's with the golden hair and eyes that open?"

"That's the one. I see she's told you about it."

"She seldom speaks of anything else — when she's talking about her birthday, I mean. She's already named it. She calls it Emmaline, but I fancy it will be plain old Emma before long. I'm so glad she'll be getting it. She would be miserable if she weren't."

After Miss Rafferty left, Rosalind thought about their brief conversation, and knew that Miss Rafferty had a genuine love and concern for her charge. Sukey would need someone like her when she, Rosalind, removed to London. It would be wretched if Annabelle insisted on turning her off.

They left for Croydon at three, in the family carriage. A footman accompanied Miss Lovelace to the drapery shop and waited while she selected silk stockings, new gloves, and a few personal items to refresh her toilette. Half an hour after she arrived, Miss Rafferty and Sukey came in and the footman took the parcels to the carriage.

Miss Rafferty, her eyes gleaming, said in a low voice, "I have discovered the very thing to please her, Miss Lovelace. It's so simple I ought to have thought of it myself. A set of crayons and a drawing book. Her crayons are all worn down to nubs. It will be something to amuse her on a rainy day."

"You run back and buy them, and I shall watch her."

Rosalind let Sukey choose her ribbons — blue to match her eyes, and a shorter length for Snow Drop — then took her out to meet Miss Rafferty.

"Did you get them?" Sukey asked, looking at the bag in her governess's hand.

"Aren't you the nosy Parker!" Miss Rafferty replied. "If you must know, I got a notebook for you to write out lines when you don't do your lessons."

"You did not," Sukey said, unfazed. "Can I have an ice before we go home?"

"May I?" Miss Rafferty corrected.

"That's what I'm asking you," Sukey said.

"Yes, you may. And I shall have a cup of tea while you youngsters have your ice," Rosalind said, and they began walking along the busy street to the tea parlor.

"Oh, Miss Lovelace," Miss Rafferty said. "Wouldn't you rather have an ice? You can have tea any time at home."

"Tea for me."

Again Rosalind was struck with the notion that she had indeed outgrown her first youth. Like the older ladies, it was a cup of tea that she craved, not an ice. The little shop was bustling with afternoon shoppers stopping for a break. The crowd was composed mostly of ladies, but there were a few blue jackets amid the throng. They chose a table close to the window and placed their orders. Several ladies stopped for a word with Rosalind and Miss Rafferty. All expressed their pleasure at Sylvia's new position and told Miss Lovelace how fortunate she was to have got her.

Sukey, not much interested in these chats, looked around the shop and made a surprising discovery. "There is Annabelle and Silly Sylvester, having an ice," she said.

"Lord Sylvester has gone to London," Rosalind said.

"No, he hasn't. He's having an ice with Annabelle. I'm going to tell Dick on her."

Rosalind had her back to the couple. It was Miss Rafferty who confirmed it.

"It is Miss Fortescue, and with a smart-looking gent." She had never seen Lord Sylvester.

"It's him," Sukey said. "They're leaving. Good!"

Annabelle spotted Sukey and the others on the way out and stopped to have a word with them. "Rosalind," she said, smiling triumphantly and sliding her arm through Sylvester's.

"Miss Lovelace," Sylvester added, bowing to the table and turning pink about the ears. "As you see, I am still here." He emitted a nervous little laugh, almost a giggle.

"Yes, so I see," Rosalind replied, and introduced Miss Rafferty.

"The party lasted so late last evening that I slept late this morning, nearly till lunch," Sylvester said. As it was now almost five o'clock, however, this did not explain his still being in town.

Annabelle felt no embarrassment at all. "And I convinced him to stay for the day. Lord Sylvester has taken me to the bookshop to help me choose some really worthwhile books. I am tired of silly Gothic novels."

Before Rosalind could think of a reply, Annabelle turned to Miss Rafferty. "Out enjoying yourself *again*, Miss Rafferty? My, weren't you fortunate to find such an undemanding employer? What is the excuse this time?"

"Tomorrow is Sukey's birthday," Miss Rafferty replied.

"And you are celebrating a day early?"

Rosalind willed down a sharp retort and said, "I asked Miss Rafferty to join me, as I wished to bring Sukey to town to choose a present."

"I hope you bought her something educational," Annabelle sniffed.

"You must agree she is a little young for really worthwhile books, as you are only beginning to read them now," Rosalind replied.

Over Annabelle's shoulder, Lord Sylvester gave Rosalind a conspiratorial smile and tried to pour oil on the troubled waters. "So you have a birthday tomorrow, eh, Miss Sukey?" he said in a hearty manner. "Well, as I shan't be here, let me wish you a happy one now."

Sukey just stared at him.

"Say 'Thank you', Sukey," Miss Rafferty said.

"Thank you," Sukey said, and shoveled another spoonful of the ice into her mouth.

"Well, I daresay we ought to be getting along, Miss Fortescue," Sylvester said.

"Tell Dick to call on me this evening, Rosalind," Annabelle said, with a long, hard look at Miss Rafferty. "I would like to have a word with him."

Angered at the chit's bold command, Rosalind replied, "I shall give him your order, but I cannot guarantee his obedience."

"He had better be there!"

Sylvester cleared his throat. "Come along, Miss Fortescue," he said. Then he forced another nervous smile, bowed again at the ladies, and left.

"I hate her," Sukey said.

126

"Ladies don't hate people," Miss Rafferty said with very little feeling. "You'd better be nice to her. She's going to be your sister."

"I already have a sister. I'm going to London to live with Roz. If you don't take me, Roz, I'll run away."

"Then you'll be sorry, Miss Lovelace!" Miss Rafferty added, and laughed.

"Can I have another ice?" Sukey asked.

"No, you may not," her sister said. "You'll spoil your dinner. Let us go, Miss Rafferty."

As they walked along to the carriage, Miss Rafferty said, "I get the feeling Miss Fortescue is unhappy with me. Would you know why, Miss Lovelace? I'm sure I've never been anything but civil to her. My job will be a hard one if the new mistress takes me in dislike."

Rosalind hardly knew what to say. "I believe she thinks Sukey should have an older governess," she said.

"Surely she doesn't think I have Mr Lovelace in my eye?"

"Perhaps she's worried at having a pretty young lady about the house. You know how new brides are."

"I never thought of myself as pretty! I'm a regular hedgehog beside her. Who would look twice at me when he had Miss Fortescue?"

"Oh, I think you're pretty," Rosalind said, and frowned. Too pretty!

After a moment's silence, Miss Rafferty said, "Should I be looking about for another position, do you think? I love working at Apple Hill, but if I'm causing trouble, I'll leave. It does seem a pity, when Sukey and I get along so well."

"I shouldn't do anything before the wedding," Rosalind said, and smiled in sympathy. She could not in good conscience give more hope than that.

It really was too bad of Annabelle, but there was little doubt that Miss Rafferty's life would be a living hell once Annabelle took over the house.

All the ladies were quiet on the way home. Sukey leaned against Rosalind's shoulder and dozed. Miss Rafferty worried over her future, and Rosalind wondered exactly why Sylvester was still in Croydon. Yesterday he had been in a great hurry to get to London. Now he could afford a whole day to help Annabelle select "really worthwhile books," which she would probably not even open once he was gone, but would display on the sofa table to impress callers.

Clearly Annabelle, with her great hankering for titles, was trying to impress Sylvester. Rosalind decided that he was only trying to get more money from Fortescue for *Camena*, but he might at least have told her he was still in town. It had been embarrassing to meet him with Annabelle. How Harry would laugh if he found out. As to what Dick would say to Annabelle's bold command, she didn't even like to think.

When she spoke to Dick later, she softened the command to a request and added, "If you are not too busy."

"I can't visit her tonight. My mare is due any hour. Her teats are wet. I'll be in the barn with the groom. Did she say what she wanted?"

"I believe she was unhappy to see Miss Rafferty in town. I invited Miss Rafferty to go with me."

128

"Does she think we ought to keep the girl a prisoner? Demmed nonsense."

"Perhaps you could send her a note."

"I suppose I must," he said. "I shall invite her to Sukey's birthday party. That might put her back in humor."

But it would spoil Sukey's party. Oh well, she would have all her gifts at least. "We planned a little tea party outdoors in the afternoon. If she could come around four . . ."

Dick nodded. "She was with Lord Sylvester, did you say?"

"Yes. He was helping her choose some books."

"I hope he's not coming to Sukey's party!"

"No, he will be gone to London."

"Thank God for that," Dick said, and went off to his study to write the note.

Rosalind felt a sense of relief at the thought of his departure as well and told herself it had nothing to do with Sylvester himself. He was delightful company. It was just that he did not mix well with provincials.

CHAPTER
FOURTEEN

The day of Sukey's birthday dawned fair. The sky was that dazzling blue that urged birds from their nests to wheel and soar in its glory. A zephyr stirred the leafy branches. Dick smiled as he tiptoed to the nursery to place his present on the table, so that Sukey might have the day's enjoyment from it. It was a new saddle for her pony, Gully. The saddle was of tan leather, embossed and studded with brass beads arranged in a swirling pattern.

Sukey came pelting downstairs from the nursery while Dick was just finishing his breakfast. She threw her arms around him and placed a loud kiss on his cheek.

"Thanks, Dick. It's just what I wanted! How did you guess?"

"It was your pointing it out to me every time we passed the saddler's shop that tipped me the clue."

Miss Rafferty came behind her, carrying the saddle.

Dick leapt up from the table, nearly upsetting his cup. "Miss Rafferty, you shouldn't be carrying that. It's too heavy for a lady."

She laughed away his concern. "I've carried heavier loads than this in my life. It's a grand saddle, Mr Lovelace. You're a lucky girl, Miss Sukey."

130

Dick took it from her and called a servant to take it out to the stable. He finished his coffee and left with Sukey. He wanted to see it placed on the pony's back and watch Sukey take her first ride on it.

"It seems you will have the morning free, Miss Rafferty," Rosalind said. "You won't be able to get Sukey out of the saddle if I know anything. A groom will be with her. I see you wisely had her wear her riding habit."

"Bessie, from the kitchen, told me what Mr Lovelace was giving her for a present. When the day was so fine, I knew how she would spend the morning. Since it's her birthday, I think we might spare her her lessons, eh? Can I give you a hand preparing her party, Miss Lovelace?"

"I'd appreciate it, if you have no chores of your own to attend to. We'll go outside after breakfast and choose a spot for the table. Sit down and join me for coffee."

Miss Rafferty smiled her pleasure and sat beside Rosalind. "There's one thing I wanted to ask you, ma'am. About Sukey's party . . ."

"Yes, what is it?"

Miss Rafferty moistened her lips, then blurted it out. "Will I be going to the party? I mean — Sukey expects me to, but if Miss Fortescue is to come, I doubt she'll welcome me. Is she coming?"

"Dick invited her, but of course, you will come," Rosalind said at once. She felt the blood rise at the very question, or rather, at the possible troubles ahead. Yet it was only right that Miss Rafferty should attend this special do for her charge. Rosalind's governesses had always attended her birthday parties. Sukey would want it, Dick would want it, and Rosalind wanted it, too.

Miss Rafferty still looked leery. "I could say I have the megrims if my being there is likely to stir up a hornet's nest. I wouldn't want to do anything to spoil Sukey's party."

The ladies exchanged a tacit but extremely conscious look. They both knew the party would already be spoiled if Annabelle attended. One could not but compare the natures of the two ladies concerned — Miss Rafferty so eager to ensure peace and harmony, and Annabelle so bent on destroying it. Miss Rafferty had glided into the tempo of life at Apple Hill so easily and naturally that she already seemed like one of the family. How would they ever get on without her?

"Perhaps she won't come," Miss Rafferty said. "No point meeting trouble halfway, as my nanny used to say."

"I would like you to come," Rosalind said firmly. "Miss Fortescue is not mistress of this house yet."

"If you say so, ma'am, but I really meant my offer to have the megrims."

They abandoned this prickly subject and enjoyed the remainder of their coffee in discussing local matters. When they were finished, they went outside to choose a spot for the party.

"There, beneath the mulberry tree, is where I would choose," Miss Rafferty said. "It's not too far for the servants to have to cart everything. It will give us shade if the sun is hot, and shelter from a light sprinkle. That breeze is picking up. I hope it doesn't rain on the cake."

Again Miss Rafferty's good common sense was revealed, and her concern for the household servants, which was always a feature of life at Apple Hill, where the servants were considered part of the family.

They spent a busy hour overseeing the setting up of the party facilities, then went around to the meadow to watch Sukey riding proudly on her new saddle. Snow Drop did not care for horses. It was Sandy who trailed behind Gully, barking his pleasure. Dick was still there, watching her and calling instructions.

"Doesn't she ride well!" Miss Rafferty exclaimed. "Oh, I wish I could ride. I've never had the opportunity."

"We have a spare hack in the stable," Dick said. "Feel free to use it, Miss Rafferty."

"That's very kind of you, sir," she said.

But the look she exchanged with Rosalind said, Don't worry. I won't do it. *She* wouldn't like it.

After lunch, the ladies made a special toilette for the party. Rosalind wore the gown with the lowered neckline and a leghorn straw bonnet with a broad brim to protect her from the sun. When Miss Rafferty brought Sukey down, both ladies were in their best afternoon frocks. Sukey looked unusually ladylike in a white dress with a wide blue sash and her new blue hair ribbons holding back her curls. She carried Snow Drop, who had a matching blue ribbon around her neck for the occasion. Miss Rafferty had blossomed forth from her usual dark governess's clothes into a jonquil muslin with green ribbons, and a straw bonnet.

Dick looked at her, then took a second look. He didn't smile, but he gazed at her long enough to betray that he hadn't missed a single ribbon, or the fact that her brown eyes were glowing and her curls gleaming like freshly peeled chestnuts in the sunlight.

"You all look lovely," he said, then he formally offered Sukey his arm and led the party down to the table, where a pile of presents loomed enticingly.

A guest was already there awaiting them. Lord Harwell sat at his ease, sorting through the gifts. He rose, bowed formally to Sukey, and said, "Many happy returns of the day, Miss Sukey." Then he handed her a small box wearing a pink ribbon.

"I thought you'd forget," she said. Then she added nonchalantly over her shoulder, "I invited Harry, Roz."

Harwell glanced at the five places at the table and said, "Is this fifth place for me, or should I claim a pressing engagement elsewhere?"

"Don't be silly," Rosalind said, and sent the servant off for another place setting.

"Annabelle is still to come, is she?" he said. "Odd she sent her present on in advance. I've been examining the offerings. Hers looks like a book. Not what I would have expected from her."

"She sent the present?" Rosalind said, and went to examine it. "Yes, definitely a book. Is there a card? Perhaps she's not coming." She exchanged a small, hopeful, spontaneous smile with Miss Rafferty. She looked around and found a card stuck to the back of the gift.

134

Harwell lifted an eyebrow and said in a quiet aside, "You sound positively hopeful, Roz. Have you and Miss Fortescue come to cuffs so soon?"

"Not yet. Truth to tell, however, we are never far from it. I shall open this card, as Sukey — to her shame — can't read." She looked at the envelope. "Oh, it's addressed to Dick."

She gave the card to Dick, who opened it, read the message, and folded it up again with a grim set to his lips. "Annabelle can't make it," he said. "Pity. Her papa had to go up to London on business, and she went with him to do some shopping. She wishes you a happy birthday, Sukey."

Rosalind assumed his annoyance was because Sylvester had also gone to London. She felt a stab of anger herself. Really, Annabelle was too encroaching, scrambling off to London after Sylvester.

"I didn't invite *her*!" Sukey said. Then she said to Miss Rafferty in a perfectly audible aside, "I'm glad she can't come. What did she send me?"

"Time to open the gifts," Rosalind said, hoping to divert Dick's attention. He looked ready to give Sukey a scold.

Sukey tore the ribbons off Annabelle's gift and looked at it in disgust. It was a thin volume, covered in morocco leather with gilt lettering. *Summer Solstice — The Nature Poems of Lord Sylvester Staunton*. Sukey flipped through it. "It doesn't have any pictures!" she said. "What does it say?"

Dick glanced at the card. "It says it is a very rare copy of a limited edition of poems that should be put away as it will be very valuable one day. I daresay he only had a dozen of them printed up at his own expense."

"I hate poems!" Sukey said. Then she glanced apologetically at Rosalind. "Except for yours and nursery rhymes," she added, and snatched up another present.

She was enchanted with Emmaline, the golden-haired doll, and with Miss Rafferty's offering of crayons and drawing book. Snow Drop enjoyed playing with the discarded wrappings. The wind blew a ribbon across the grass, with Snow Drop in hot pursuit. Sukey opened Lord Harwell's present last.

"This doesn't look like my sugarplums, Harry. It's too small," she said, shaking the little box.

"Good things come in small parcels," he told her.

"My saddle didn't. It didn't come in a parcel at all. You never did give me the sugarplums."

"The sugarplums aren't a birthday gift. I didn't bother to wrap them," he said, pointing to a plain box on the table by her place.

She vacillated a moment between the sugarplums and the wrapped gift, then tore open the small parcel, struggled with the little leather box within, and eventually lifted out a dainty golden heart-shaped locket on a fine chain. "Jewelry!" she cried, her eyes big as saucers. "I never had any real jewelry before. Thanks, Harry!" She ran and wrapped her arms around his knees, as she could not reach his neck.

Harwell looked in alarm to see her hands were clean.

Sukey released him and said, "Put it on me, Miss Rafferty."

Miss Rafferty did as she was told.

"Don't I look nice?" Sukey asked proudly, stroking the locket.

"Fine as ninepence," Harwell assured her.

"That was very sweet, Harry," Rosalind said, smiling softly.

"I thought you might ring a peal over me for giving a young lady jewelry. I wanted to buy her a doll, but she mentioned that you were already giving her one."

"I can see my gift was a great surprise."

"Let's eat the cake now," Sukey said.

"First there are sandwiches," Miss Rafferty told her.

"I want my cake."

"And you shall have it," Dick said, "as soon as you've eaten your sandwiches."

Sukey took one bite, then fed the rest to Snow Drop.

"Where is Sandy today?" Harwell asked, looking around for the dog, which usually accompanied Sukey.

"Sandy and Snow Drop cannot seem to get along," Rosalind said. "Sandy is in the stable."

"Ah well, a showy new pet will always replace an old dog — for a while." He glanced to see if Rosalind was finding any second meaning in his speech.

"I expect it's the inability to teach old dogs any new tricks that makes us lose interest in them," she replied.

"There is a facer for me!"

"Oh, but we were only talking about dogs, Harry." She sliced the cake, and the servants passed it around. Sukey had lemonade, and the adults had wine.

"You should make a toast, Mr Lovelace," Miss Rafferty suggested.

"A toast!" Dick agreed, rising and lifting his glass. The others rose. "To Sukey's sixth birthday. May she have many more of them."

They all repeated the toast and drank. By the time the cake was consumed and a little light chat indulged in, Sukey decided she wanted to take her doll inside to play house. She did not forget to pick up her sugarplums.

"I'll go with you," Miss Rafferty said, rising. Dick accompanied them, while Rosalind stayed behind to oversee the servants, who came out to clear away the debris from the party.

"They can handle it," Harwell said. "Let us go for a little stroll, before the rain comes."

He took her arm and led her off.

CHAPTER
FIFTEEN

The azure sky of morning had lightened to pale blue by afternoon. It was now white, rapidly darkening to gray, but the storm didn't seem imminent. They walked through the park, toward the gazebo.

"A nice party," he said.

"Yes, that was a lovely gift, Harry. How did you come to think of it?"

"I remember my mama telling me her first jewelry was a golden locket from her papa. She cherished it until the day she died. As Sukey has lost her papa, I decided to give her the little trinket as a keepsake. No doubt it will end up decorating Emmaline."

"It's not like you to be sentimental," she said, but she said it in a fond, smiling way.

"Perhaps there's more to me than you know," he replied, and immediately changed the subject. "Did Sylvester get off to London all right?"

"Yes. Actually he remained a day at Fortescue's but has gone on to London now."

"I noticed him buttering up Fortescue at the party. Did he get any money out of him?"

"A thousand pounds."

"That should stave off bankruptcy for a few more months. The fellow could sell ice to Esquimaux. But then, I don't have to tell you what a salesman he is," he said quizzingly. "You've bought his goods."

"On the contrary, he's bought mine," she retorted.

When they reached the gazebo, a Gothic structure of old stone, he took her elbow to lead her up the stairs. She looked up at the darkening sky and said, "I ought to be getting back before the rain comes. You don't have to walk me home, Harry. Just cut through the park to the Abbey. Or did you ride?"

"I walked, and I shall walk you home." He peered down at her and said archly, "What was that about not being able to teach an old dog new tricks? I am no longer the ramshackle sort of fellow who abandons a lady in distress."

"Just as well. I used to be your cohort in the old days. I shall no longer be here to abet you. I am not in distress, however, but I shall be if I get caught here in the rain. If you insist on playing the gentleman, let us go on home." They headed to the house.

"Still determined to go to London?" he asked, taking her arm in an effort to slow her dash.

She looked at him in surprise. "Yes, certainly. Nothing has happened to change my mind."

"Dick tells me Miss Fortescue has taken poor Miss Rafferty in violent dislike. I cannot imagine why. She seems the ideal governess. My thinking is that Sukey will need you if she loses Miss Rafferty. Sukey makes no secret of her dislike of Dick's choice of bride."

140

"I doubt Dick will turn Miss Rafferty off. Annabelle is becoming overbearing in her behavior."

"Dick showed me her note. Have you read it?"

"No. Is there something in it —"

"An ultimatum. Turn Miss Rafferty off, or else. He thinks this jaunt to London is to trim him into line. It seems Dick failed to show up for a date last night."

"It was no date! She demanded that he go. He didn't oblige her." She shook her head in vexation. "I oughtn't to be discussing these things outside the family."

"Don't be a ninny. We've discussed more intimate secrets than this before now, Roz."

"Yes, and I know I can trust your discretion." They stopped a moment by a rustic bench but didn't sit down. "The thing is, Annabelle is jealous of Miss Rafferty, I think. Not entirely without reason. Dick is fond of her. Not that there is anything improper going on! But a natural affection is growing, perhaps into something more."

He looked at her a long moment, with what looked like pity, or some tender emotion. "Yes, I see how that could happen," he said softly.

"It is hardly surprising, I suppose. Miss Rafferty is so thoughtful, and very pretty, too, in her own quiet way." She opened her budget, for she wanted some more objective person to discuss it with, and could think of no one more suitable than Harry, her oldest and dearest friend.

"Any possibility of Annabelle's calling the wedding off?" he asked.

"You think the marriage is a bad idea, then?" she asked eagerly.

"I wouldn't have the wench if she came with all the gold in the mint. An underbred, scolding nag — and that before the wedding! Only imagine what a tyrant she will grow into once she is mistress."

"I'm glad to hear you say it. I thought it was only I who felt this way — because of her dangling after Sylvester, you know. Not that he cares for her in the least. It is the papa he is courting."

"Hardly an endearing quality."

"Oh, but for *Camena*! It is not for himself. He cares nothing for money. But really this is not about Sylvester. It is about Dick and Annabelle. I think Dick is beginning to realize what a mistake he's made. But how can he get out of it? The man cannot cry off."

"You say she's adamant that you leave Apple Hill. If you stayed . . ."

"No," she said firmly. "Dick is a man now. Let him solve his own problems. It's not for me to handle them — and what would I get for my pains? As soon as Annabelle was turned off, he would decide he loved her after all. I am always the one who puts her foot down, and look where it's got me. Annabelle won't have me in the house. Everyone thinks me a shrew, always carping and scolding."

"Someone's got to do it."

"It doesn't always have to be me. Dick has got to do it this time. It is his problem."

As she spoke, she spotted Dick striding toward them. His angry scowl announced trouble. She noticed he was carrying a white card. Annabelle's note, she felt sure.

"I didn't want to spoil the party," he said, "but have a look at this, if you please."

Rosalind took the card with trembling fingers and read:

Dear Dick:

Sorry I cannot make Sukey's party. I have gone up to London with Papa to begin shopping for my trousseau. While I am gone, I wish you to dispense with Miss Rafferty's services. I will not have that woman in my house. As you are dead set against sending Sukey to school as you ought, perhaps she and Miss Rafferty could make their home in London with Rosalind? Just a thought. See you tomorrow.

Love, Annabelle.

"*Her* house!" Dick said, fulminating. "Upon my word, she goes too far. It ain't her house yet. First she orders you out, then Miss Rafferty, now Sukey. I begin to wonder how long she will allow me to remain. Or how long I will want to."

"If you are waiting for me to say I will take Sukey and Miss Rafferty to London —"

"Dash it, that's not what I'm saying. This is Sukey's home."

"Then what?"

"We've got to tell her who runs things here."

"No, Dick. *You* have got to tell her. I shan't be here to tame Annabelle for you after you are married. Begin as you mean to go on."

"Truth to tell, I thought it would be getting rid of you that would be the problem."

Rosalind's nostrils thinned in annoyance. "I'm glad I could help you there."

"It ain't a help."

"What are you saying?"

"I don't want to marry her. Dash it, ever since the betrothal, she's turned into a demmed shrew. How can I get out of it if you leave?"

"I don't know, Dick. It is your problem. You're the master of Apple Hill. It's time you grew up and looked after yourself — and Sukey."

Dick first looked offended. Then he straightened his shoulders, assumed a mannish air, and said, "So it is. You have kept me a boy too long." He turned abruptly on his heel and strode manfully toward the house.

Rosalind looked after him with a wistful expression on her face, then she looked at Harwell, who was smiling cynically.

"There's gratitude for you," he said. "*You* have kept him a boy."

"What really hurts is that it's true, at least in part. I've always made the hard decisions for him. I felt such a horrible urge to say I would take Sukey to London with me, but it won't do."

"This is her home."

"Yes, what would there be for her to do in London? She is so happy here, with her pony and dog."

"And Snow Drop."

"You remembered the name."

"Perhaps I'm growing up, too."

"Yes, everything is changing," she said, blinking away a tear, and turned to leave.

Harwell didn't follow her. He stood, watching with a bemused expression as she hurried after Dick. He found it odd that the sly, practical Annabelle would issue an ultimatum before the wedding. Why not wait until after? The wedding was only a few months away.

Was it possible she had a trick up her sleeve? And if that trick was Lord Sylvester, would it break Rosalind's heart? She was as sentimental as an adolescent, beneath that sensible exterior. If her poems hadn't told him, the tears gathering in her eyes when she left would have done it. She actually loved that popinjay. And despite her defense of him, she feared he would be seduced into offering for Fortescue's fortune.

CHAPTER
SIXTEEN

When two days passed and still Annabelle had not returned to Croydon, Dick announced that he was going to London to speak to her.

"Perhaps you should, or at least write," Rosalind replied. "It would be too bad if she wasted a fortune on a trousseau when there is to be no wedding. They usually put up at the Pulteney Hotel."

"What shall I say in my letter?"

"That you are in receipt of her note and regret you cannot oblige her. You are not turning Miss Rafferty off as she gives excellent satisfaction and would be impossible to replace. You might as well tell her I have no intention of taking Sukey to London with me while you are about it."

"I'll do it this minute," he said, and stomped to his study, murmuring, "Regret I cannot oblige you" and "Excellent satisfaction," lest he forget the words, which had exactly the haughty tone he wanted.

He had just finished the letter and brought it for Rosalind's approval when Miss Rafferty and Sukey came in. They had been to Croydon to purchase muslin for a new gown for Sukey. Sukey was her usual voluble self, but Miss Rafferty seemed strangely quiet. The parcel was opened, the pink sprigged muslin approved, and Miss Rafferty began to bundle it up to take it abovestairs.

"I have a message for you, Mr Lovelace," she said, using the excuse of the parcel to avoid meeting his look. "Miss Fortescue is back from London and wants to see you. She will be at home this evening."

"Will she, by God!" Dick said, fulminating.

Miss Rafferty looked up then, with some uncertainty, as if she would add to the message. But as she glanced at Dick, she sensed the smoke in the air and left, with a half-frightened glance over her shoulder at Rosalind. Sukey went hopping after her.

As soon as they were gone, Dick turned a wrathful face to his sister. "Summoning me again, as if I were a dashed lackey. All that writing for nothing," he said, and squeezed his letter into a ball, which he tossed into the grate.

"Go and get it over with, Dick. Better to do it face-to-face."

She let Dick talk out his anger and frustration, feeling it better he should vent his feelings at home than make a cake of himself in front of Annabelle.

"Well, I'll go, then," he said. "But I'll dashed well have my dinner first."

"Let us both go up and change now," she suggested.

Before going to her room, she went to have a word with Miss Rafferty. Rosalind sent Sukey off to the kitchen to ensure privacy.

"Mr Lovelace didn't seem very happy at my message," Miss Rafferty said, peering up from the pattern book she and Sukey had been studying to choose a pattern for the new frock.

"He is a little upset," Rosalind answered discreetly, for it would not do to become too intimate with the servants. "How did Annabelle seem?"

"Very much as usual. Oh, she was wearing a new bonnet with a great high poke, the rim all covered with flowers. It is all the crack in London, she said. Lord Sylvester helped her pick it out."

"I see," Rosalind said, damping down a flare of anger.

Miss Rafferty cast the magazine aside and said in an anxious voice, "Oh, Miss Lovelace, it hardly seems my place to deliver such a message. I hadn't the nerve to say it to Mr Lovelace, and that's a fact. She said, 'Pray tell Mr Lovelace to call on me this evening. And he had better be there, or else'. Just like that, with her nose in the air. I didn't know which way to look. She said it as loud as can be in the drapery shop, with all the old quizzes cocking an ear."

Rosalind gave a *tsk* of disgust. "Just as well you didn't tell my brother. Was there anything else?"

Miss Rafferty bit her lips and worried her fingers. "She spoke a good deal about Lord Sylvester," she admitted, with obvious reluctance. "He had taken her about here and there, it seems. To a play, and for tea at his papa's mansion. Mr Fortescue was along as well for the tea party. Oh, miss, she was so loud and brazen, I was ashamed for her. It was Lord Dunston this and Lady Dunston that, as if they were bosom bows, and she's never even laid eyes on them. They were at

148

Astonby. When she spoke of Lord Sylvester, she called him by just his Christian name, too. I sent Sukey off to look at the ribbons, for I didn't want her to hear what was being said. She might tell Mr Lovelace, you know."

"That was well done."

"I don't know if I should even be telling you all this about Lord Sylvester, though I had the feeling Miss Fortescue wanted me to."

"I'll hear it all soon enough if it was said in the drapery shop."

"Well, there's one thing clear," Miss Rafferty said, her shoulders sagging. "I'll never be able to stay on when she marries Mr Lovelace. She's taken me in dislike, though I'm sure I've never done a thing to harm her." Tears started in her eyes. She blinked and turned her head away in an effort to conceal them.

Rosalind felt such a pressure of frustration, she wanted to scream. Miss Rafferty's great crime was that Dick liked her, and who could blame him for preferring a sweet, unspoiled lady over that witch of an Annabelle? It tweaked her pride, too, that Annabelle had purloined Lord Sylvester. It was mainly her pride that was stung, however. Her attraction for the poetical lord was beginning to fade to contempt. How far would he go to find backers for his magazine?

Buttering up a rich old retired solicitor who wanted a touch of class was one thing. Leading on the wealthy man's daughter was something else. In her heart, she could not think Sylvester was doing that. He associated with a different class of people in London. Manners were freer there. Harry had said he ran with a pretty racy set, but that did not mean Sylvester was like the others. He was young, not aware of the danger inherent in fast companions. She would steer him away from that sort when she was in London.

She patted Miss Rafferty's shoulder, but disliked to make any promises she might not be able to keep. It was entirely possible Annabelle would work her charms on Dick, when she had him there in person. Perhaps a letter would have been better after all.

"We are very happy with your work, Sylvia," she said, using the first name on purpose, to show her support went beyond that of employer to embrace the role of friend.

"You'll give me a good recommendation, then?"

"If it comes to that. I sincerely hope it will not."

"Thank you, Ros — Miss Lovelace."

"You will have no trouble finding a new position."

"But not so close to home, where I can visit Mama often. I hate to think of leaving the neighborhood where I grew up and have known everyone forever." Rosalind left, to let Sylvia dry her tears in private. Her heart was heavy. No point saying it was Dick's job to sort this out. This was her home, too, and this was her problem. Sukey was her sister, as dear to her as a daughter. Dick was her only brother. If he married Annabelle, Rosalind knew she would take Sukey and Miss Rafferty to London, but she would insist Dick pay for the additional expense. And she would not tell him of her decision unless and until he announced he was definitely marrying Annabelle.

150

She thought about Miss Rafferty's words about leaving home, where she had grown up and known everyone forever. The same applied to herself. She felt a wrenching inside to think of leaving home. It would be exciting, but it would be sad, too.

She went to her room and arranged her evening toilette. The green muslin gown on which she had lowered the neckline hung crookedly on its hanger, as if ashamed of itself. She was little better than Annabelle. She, too, had made a cake of herself to gain her own ends. Dressing up and pretending she was something she was not. Letting Lord Sylvester tell her and the world her poems were something they were not. And Harry laughing his head off at her the whole time.

Why had she done it? Annabelle's shoving her out of her home was not the whole reason. It was the dull sameness of her life, the feeling that there was something better out there, in fabled London. But the people were no better than here. Indeed it seemed some of them were a deal worse. But surely there were other more worthwhile people as well? She would make a determined effort to find them — for herself and for Sylvester. She would reform him, if he was in need of reformation.

She would go to London; she owed it to herself to give it a try, but she was beginning to think of it in terms of a visit only. If Dick managed to disentangle himself from Annabelle, she would soon return to Apple Hill.

In the bottom of her heart there rested the image of Harry, walking along the path in the sunshine, cradling

Snow Drop in the crook of one arm and holding Sukey's hand on the other side. Why had she remembered that? Why did she often think of it? It had struck some deep chord in her, shown her a side of Harry she seldom saw. The gentle, thoughtful side. "Perhaps there's more to me than you know," he had said. Yet she believed she knew him pretty well after twenty-odd years.

Dinner was a tense meal. Dick ate and drank without speaking. Even the servants were subdued. It was not unheard-of for the footmen to praise Cook's work and recommend a second helping, but they moved silently that evening. The loudest sound in the room was the tinkle of cutlery on china. Rosalind knew better than to urge Dick into speech. He would only say things he shouldn't in front of the servants. He didn't bother taking port. Immediately after dinner he put on his curled beaver and went to the saloon for a word in private with his sister before leaving.

"Well, I am off," he said. "Wish me well."

She remembered his having said very much the same thing the evening he went to propose to Annabelle. He had looked the same, too. Tense, worried. Only the reek of lavender water was missing. He had showered himself with it on that other occasion. And he had come home smiling. Perhaps he would come home smiling tonight, as happy to be rid of his prize as he had been to win her.

"Don't lose your temper, Dick," was all she said. "Remember, you are a gentleman."

"If she says one word against Miss Rafferty, I daresay I shall give her a piece of my mind." On this curt speech, he turned on his heel and left.

Rosalind took up a book of poems to pass the time until Dick's return. She was sitting with the book on her knee, gazing into the cold grate, when Lord Harwell was announced. She hadn't seen him since Sukey's birthday party, but she had often thought of him.

"You're still at the Abbey, are you?" she said, as he strolled in and made a sort of casual, abbreviated bow.

"For the present. I came to see how the tangled love affair is going on. Where's Dick?"

"In Croydon. He says he is going to confront Annabelle about Sylvia Rafferty. Heaven knows what will happen."

Harwell lounged on a chair beside her and helped himself to a glass of wine. "Will you go to London if he don't marry Annabelle?"

"Yes, I plan to go, either way."

He just nodded and didn't try to dissuade her, although he seemed unhappy with her answer.

"I saw Annabelle in town this afternoon, looking very well pleased with herself," he said. "She's having a party to celebrate her papa's partnership with Sylvester. The thousand-pound merger, you know."

"Any excuse will do. It will be a boon for the flower sellers and merchants."

"And the drapery shop. I expect even Miss Lovelace may dash down to Fulton's and snap up a few ells of silk before they are gone, eh?"

"To impress young Sylvester, you mean?"

"And old Harwell," he added, smiling as his eyes lingered on her quaint gown.

They talked for half an hour about local doings, then Harwell rose. He didn't seem to have come for any other reason than to check up on Dick's romance.

"Let me know the result," he said.

"Do you really want me to send you a note?" she asked, wondering if he was just making conversation. "It's not like you to be so interested in romance."

"I'm always interested in romance."

"No, in your own flirtations. There is a difference, Harry."

"So there is. Trust a poet to note the fine points. And incidentally, there are other ways of contacting me than by writing a note. You could call on me, you know." The "incidentally" suggested his remark was an afterthought, but the way he gazed at her sent a different message. His dark eyes wore an air of injury. She waited to see if he made some joking comment, but he just went on looking.

"I see you want all the spicy details."

"Perhaps I just want you to call on me, as you used to."

Rosalind looked at him, wondering what freakish new idea he had taken into his head. "I never called on you unless you asked me to. I used to call on your mama when she was alive. What is it you want me to do for you?" she asked, instantly suspicious.

There was no ignoring his expression now. He definitely looked offended. "Is that really your opinion of me? That I only invite you to call when I want something from you? I thought we were friends."

"We are!"

"Perhaps I deserved that swat on the wrist. I shall try to do better in future."

He rose, bowed, and left before she could apologize, or ask why he had come. As she sat on alone, she felt she should be working on her poetry, but no inspiration came. She was too distraught, worrying about what was going forth at Croydon. It was another hour before she heard the door open, and Dick's footsteps approaching the saloon. She tensed, waiting for the first glance at his face, which would tell the story.

CHAPTER
SEVENTEEN

When at last Dick entered the saloon, his appearance revealed nothing to Rosalind. He was not wearing the frown that would speak of failure, nor a smile to show success. His expression was brooding, tending toward angry.

"Well?" she asked.

He sat down, shoved his hands in his trouser pockets, stuck his long legs straight out in front of him, and scowled at his slippers. "Nothing has been settled," he said, and drew one hand out of his pocket to reach for the wine decanter.

"But that's impossible. What happened? What did you say? What did she say?"

"I said Miss Rafferty was an excellent governess and I was not about to turn her off on Annabelle's say-so. She said she would have to think about that. It is a lady's prerogative, she says."

"How very odd!" And how very disappointing.

"Yes, I was braced to be met with tears and accusations that I didn't love her, or even one of her dashed temper tantrums, but there was nothing of the sort. She just looked — smug. I couldn't get her to budge an inch. I came the heavy in fine form. 'I am the master in my own home', I told her. 'Perhaps you are right, Dick', she said, nice as a nun, but with such a sly glint in her eyes, I could see she didn't mean a word of it."

"How long does she expect her thinking to take?"

"She says she will tell me on Saturday evening, after the party. Did I mention she is having another party?"

"Harry was here. He told me."

"I got one concession out of her at least. She says Miss Rafferty will be invited to the do, as I am so exceedingly fond of her. That is the way she put it. It was all I could do to keep my tongue between my teeth."

"As if Miss Rafferty would go with that sort of invitation!"

"What is she up to, Roz? You're a woman. You must know."

"I haven't the faintest notion. That mention of your being so fond of Miss Rafferty is hardly conciliating, yet it seems she isn't ready to give you up yet." Even as she spoke, Annabelle's scheme began to reveal itself. She was paving the way for a jilting, but waiting until after the party to do it. She actually thought she had a chance of nabbing Sylvester! "Will Lord Sylvester be at the party?" she asked.

"Oh, certainly. It is another do in his honor, to judge by the way she speaks. She was invited to tea at his papa's house and could scarcely speak of anything but Lord Dunston, though he wasn't even there. If her papa had not been along, I would have used the tea party for an excuse to turn her off."

"She's trying to weasel a proposal out of Sylvester, Dick. That's what she is about."

"He's welcome to her, but I don't count on her success. He is only after her papa's blunt to waste on his magazine. Fortescue is too hard-headed to throw it away when he worked so hard for every penny of it. The vicar had trouble squeezing ten guineas out of him to help with repairing the stained-glass windows in the church. So we are no farther ahead than when I left." He set down his glass and said, "I say! You ain't cut up about her dangling after Lord Sylvester, are you?"

Rosalind was too frustrated to reply. She just made a batting motion of denial with her fingers.

"She'll catch cold at that. Anyhow, we have wasted enough time thinking about it," Dick said. "If you are going up to London, you had best go over the accounts with me, and tell me what I must do in future. Annabelle would be a help there at least. She always had a head for figures."

They went to his study and worked for an hour, but were both so distracted they felt it a waste of time. Dick went out to the stable to admire the foal — it was a filly — and Rosalind went up to her room to try to lose her worries in poetry. She found her thoughts turning to Harwell's odd visit and wondered if she should let him know the outcome of Dick's talk with Annabelle. Was he serious that she should call on him? It was an odd feature of their friendship that, although he ran quite tame at Apple Hill, she never went to the Abbey without an invitation. This was usually to a large party, but occasionally he wanted her help to entertain some demanding relative, or give some pushing lady the notion he was taken.

The cards to Annabelle's party arrived the next morning, including one for Miss Rafferty, who, with frightened eyes, held it in her hand as if it were a loaded pistol.

"I could never face her, Miss Lovelace," she said. "Not after the way she spoke to me." A noble look was on her face when she announced, "I shall send in a refusal."

"Do what you think best," Rosalind said, knowing Miss Rafferty was dying to go, but fearing the price to be paid. Annabelle wouldn't think twice of airing her dirty laundry in public.

Rosalind went for a ride in the afternoon to escape the house and to take out her frustrations in physical exertion. Some years ago she had dispensed with a groom for rides around her brother's property and the fields of the neighboring Abbey. It was only when she rode into town that she bothered with the proprieties. It would not do for Miss Lovelace, of Apple Hill, to enter town unescorted.

The day was fine. Billows of soft white clouds, too lazy to move, lolled in the blue heavens. The sweet aromas of summer rose from the wildflowers as she passed. Rooks nagged at her from treetops. A crystal stream gurgled by, with flashes of silver where a school of tiny fish, hardly an inch long, were rushed along with the current.

She was undecided whether to call on Harwell. In the distance the walls of the Abbey rose in ancient glory, the stone warmed by the sun. Gothic windows, their colored splendor replaced by ordinary glass centuries ago, reflected the sun's gold. On an impulse, she decided to call on Harry, but when she reached the stable, the groom told her his lordship had called for his curricle an hour before and had not returned. She was half-relieved. In her present mood, she would not be good company.

When she returned home, the butler told her Lord Harwell had been to call. He did not say whether he would return. It was one more petty annoyance to add to the unpleasant day, with everything up in the air. It would have helped relieve the tension to talk it over with Harry after all. Dick glowered when she met him in the hall. Miss Rafferty's eyes were red when Rosalind went to the schoolroom to see how Sukey was going on.

"Miss Rafferty has got a cinder in her eye," Sukey explained. "Can I go out and play now, Roz? I've done a whole page of letters. This is an *a*," she said, proudly displaying her handiwork. "And this is a *b*. It sounds like boy and bag and bug. I'm learning to read!"

"That's wonderful, Sukey. Yes, why don't you go out and ride your pony for a while. It's a lovely day." She knew the groom would see Sukey was accompanied.

The Lovelaces' socializing had increasingly centered around the Fortescues since Dick's engagement. Regular dinner parties with their old friends were less frequent. Annabelle was bored by their provincial neighbors. With the new coolness between the young couple, Rosalind and Dick had the evening to themselves. Harwell did not call.

She thought Sylvester might send her a note, but the morning brought no letter with the familiar writing. Annabelle did not call, nor did she receive calls from either of the Lovelaces, but when Rosalind drove into Croydon from sheer boredom to call on an old friend of the family, she heard plenty about the coming party. It seemed the shops and High Street were abuzz with it.

The London coach had delivered dozens of large parcels for Miss Fortescue, which were duly picked up by footmen and carried to the gaudy mansion.

Every retired and unemployed servant in town was pressed into temporary service in preparation for the event.

"They will be serving turtle soup!" Miss Vickers informed Rosalind, when they sat to have tea. This was a great innovation for local society, requiring as it did a live turtle. "Miss Spender has spent every afternoon at their house making a new gown for Mrs Fortescue. She bought the ecru taffeta and matching lace at Fulton's. Miss Fortescue had her gown made in London!" she announced, as if London were Paris, or the Far East. "She has sworn her dresser to secrecy, as if they were planning to overthrow the king, so we have not heard what the gown is like, but the servants say she has had a pair of dancing slippers dyed Olympian blue."

This suggested not only that the secret gown was blue, but that there was to be dancing. This had been in doubt as the local musicians had not been hired. It seemed that London was to supply not only the gown but the music.

Rosalind did not share these nuggets with Dick. Any mention of Annabelle sent him into a fit of the blue devils. She would have liked to discuss the coming party with someone, but it seemed cruel to tantalize Miss Rafferty when she had found the fortitude to send in her refusal to the grandest party the parish had ever seen.

Rosalind did not plan to put herself to the bother and expense of a new gown, nor would it have been possible if she had. Every modiste in town was working day and night to outfit the privileged group who had received an invitation. With no new gown to distinguish her, she was toying with the notion of sporting a turban, concocted from a leftover length of the rose silk that had been used for her new gown. Turbans looked rather modish on older ladies like herself. But then she would look like Sylvester's mama or maiden aunt. Why didn't he write?

The next morning the long-awaited letter finally arrived. It was written in a lively style, lengthy and full of plans for her remove to London. Any vague doubts and worries about Sylvester's character and intentions vanished as she read it. The flat was ready for occupancy. The sooner she could come, the better. He was most eager to show her off.

He had drawn a floor plan of the apartment where she was to live and a map of the surrounding facilities: shops, circulating libraries, churches, and so on. He had marked the homes of various friends and business associates with an X and mentioned which of them were sociable. Sir George Kingsley, it seemed, gave grand parties. A Miss Langtry was marked with a notation that she would show Rosalind around the shops, modistes, coiffeurs, etc. That was well done of him. Imagination painted a rosy future of gadding about London with the literary set. The tone of the letter left no doubt that he considered himself as her special friend, if not yet her lover.

All her early enthusiasm for the plan was reactivated. It would do her the world of good to get away. She could hardly wait.

What he had not included was the rather important matter of the flat's price. There were two paragraphs discussing her new set of poems, with voluminous suggestions as to classical references. He said he looked forward to seeing her on Saturday but did not actually say he would call. Did he mean he would see her at Annabelle's party? Not a word regarding his having squired Annabelle about London. It obviously meant nothing to him. He had only done it from gratitude for Fortescue's contribution to *Camena*.

Altogether it was a most satisfying missive and was signed "with warmest regards, Sylvester". A postscript crowded on to the bottom of the page mentioned he hoped she was not planning to bring Sukey, as London was no place for a child. She was glad she hadn't said anything to Dick about taking Sukey with her. Really Sukey would be better off at home.

Rosalind carried the letter in her pocket and was perusing it again that afternoon in the garden when

Lord Harwell came to call. He spotted her on his way from the stable to the house. She stuffed it back into her pocket and arranged a smile to greet him.

"Not a word about the mountain coming to Muhammad, sir!" she said saucily. "I called on you the other day, and you were out."

"So John Groom told me. I wonder we didn't meet on the road. I was here, calling on you." Something in her attitude called to mind that earlier meeting, when he had just returned from London. The setting was similar, with the garden all around. Her face had the same glow. On that other occasion, it was the publication of her poems that excited her, but that thrill had worn off by now. Harwell had a sinking sensation it was Sylvester who accounted for this new excitement.

"I rode through the fields, which would account for it," she said. "You have come to learn the outcome of Dick's visit to Croydon. I fear nothing has been settled."

"I already know that. Next to the party, it is the most discussed *on dit* in Croydon."

"But we haven't told anyone!"

"I wonder who did," he asked, and gave a disparaging shake of his head. This was no real mystery. The only other person who knew was Annabelle herself. "Poor Miss Rafferty features as the villainess of the piece. Dick is not fighting off her advances as he ought. A most unlikely 'other woman'. There will be fur flying before the night is over."

"It will not be Miss Rafferty's fur. She has sent in her refusal."

"A wise precaution, though it is a pity she must miss the do. It is being spoken of, even in London."

"Have you been to London?" she asked, surprised.

"Yes, I had the estate agent show me over Lord Dunston's new block of flats while I was there. A concerned neighbor's privilege. They are very handsome. Everything done up in the first style."

"And the location very convenient. Sylvester enclosed a map in his letter."

His eyes moved unconsciously to her pocket. "Is that what you were perusing so intently when I arrived?"

"I was glancing at it, yes. The flat seems ideal. I am most eager to be off. Spread my wings and fly away."

When Harwell saw the pleasure glowing in her eyes, he felt a profound sense of loss. He knew it was not a flat that put that flush on her cheeks. She was in love with the popinjay, as surely as he was in love with her. How had he not realized it years ago? The right woman was here, under his nose, all the time he had been racketing around, looking for love. He had been blinded by their friendship, but to have a lover and friend in one was the best love of all.

"About the flat, much depends on one's neighbors, of course," he said. And some of those flats had been let to dashers he would not care to see Rosalind associate with.

"I hardly think lowlifes will be able to afford such finery."

"Nor starving artists either. That was the sort of neighborhood he mentioned, was it not?"

"Other writing friends of his live nearby. It is a sort of cultural oasis. The group is close. They go about to lectures and parties and so on together. The offices of *Camena* are only a short distance away as well."

"If you find it does not suit, you will remember my offer to stay at my house. Until you find something you like better at least. I told my housekeeper she was to make you welcome if you chose to go there."

"That was — thoughtful of you," she said. As far as Rosalind was concerned, it was also unnecessary. In fact, it was bordering on the intrusive. "But I hardly think Lord Sylvester would recommend rooms that were unsuitable in any way. He knows me pretty well. He knows what would suit me."

"As Annabelle has given them her seal of approval, we must assume they do not lack for finery."

Rosalind's eyes glittered dangerously. Annabelle had approved them! Sylvester had not mentioned that! No doubt the hussy had nagged him into it.

"How soon will you be leaving?" he asked.

"Eager to be rid of me?" she snipped. Her anger was with Annabelle, but it was Harwell who was there to take the brunt of it.

"Not at all. My intention was to give a dinner party before your departure, to thank you for the many favors you've done me over the years."

She was sorry for her little outburst. "You don't have to do that, Harry."

"You mustn't expect anything on the scale of Annabelle's extravaganza."

"What, no turtle soup?" she asked with a moue.

166

He found it odd that she should adopt this coquettish attitude now, when she had chosen Sylvester. If she had behaved like this any time over the past decade, he would have realized he loved her. "That would require a week's advance notice. When will you be leaving?"

"As soon as possible. Sylvester is very eager. And so am I. To get on with our work, I mean," she added, blushing. "It would be nice if you could have the dinner party while he is here. You don't really know him very well, Harry. I would like you two to get to know one another better."

This confirmed that she was serious about the demmed fop, but at least he hadn't offered yet, or she would not have bothered with that prevarication about getting on with their work. "I know him as well as I want to, but if it would please you, then let us make it the day after Annabelle's party. Should I invite her as well?"

After a frowning pause, she said, "That will depend on what she says to Dick tomorrow evening at her party. Perhaps we should wait and see. She is hoping for an offer from Sylvester, but I fear she hopes in vain."

"You think that is what she has in mind?"

"Why else did she set that date as the time she would give Dick her answer? She is very sly, but I fear she is out in her reckoning if she thinks to buy Lord Sylvester with a thousand pounds."

"Her dowry is considerably more than that, I think?"

167

"How you harp on money! Sylvester is a poet. Money is not that important to him — except to keep *Camena* afloat, I mean."

Harwell didn't shake his head, as he wanted to. He just looked and listened, with a great weight pressing on his heart. As her talk was all of Sylvester and *Camena* and London, he soon said, "I have to be going now. I have an appointment at the Abbey," and left.

Rosalind remained in the garden, musing over her letter.

CHAPTER
EIGHTEEN

The major impediment to Rosalind's happiness on the day of the party was that when Sylvester failed to offer for Annabelle, as, of course, he would, then Annabelle would not jilt Dick. Rosalind mentioned her fear to Dick, who frowned in confusion.

"Why wouldn't he offer for her? She has bushels of blunt. He is staying at her papa's house. The Fortescues went with him to London. It's clear as a pikestaff she's nabbed him."

"I rather think Lord Sylvester is interested in me, Dick," she explained.

"You! Surely you jest. You wouldn't marry that young Jack Dandy."

"I might, if he offered."

"Good God! All that poetry has rotted your mind. As if leaving Apple Hill for London weren't bad enough, now you speak of marrying Sylvester Staunton. I would as lief see you marry Jack Ketch."

"I'm sorry you don't approve. In fact, I have not decided to have him. The point is, I don't think for a moment Sylvester is going to offer for Annabelle."

"Then we'll have to get someone else to do it. By Jove! Harry! He'll do."

"Harry!" she gasped. "Are you mad? He'd never marry her. She is the last person he'd marry."

"High time the old benedict settled down. And she has the blunt, remember. It must cost Harry a fortune to run the Abbey."

Rosalind felt a pronounced revulsion for this match. To have Miss Fortescue lording over the neighborhood as milady, littering the Abbey with her notions of finery — the thought was obscene.

"Even if he didn't actually offer, he could make up to her, let on he was interested," Dick said, as he recalled that Harry had never seemed very fond of Annabelle. "I'll suggest it to him. She'll go along with it. Mad for a title."

"No! She might manage to nab him!"

"What's that to us? You'll be in London. I'll be here with Sukey — and Miss Rafferty." He could not quite control the little smile that twitched at his lips.

"I would sooner see her marry Sylvester than Harry," Rosalind said, and strode angrily from the room with her heart banging like a hammer on an anvil. The very idea!

She had always known Harry would marry one day. Probably one day soon, as he was edging into his thirties. Every June 4 when he returned from the Season, she braced herself to hear he was engaged to some fine lord's well-dowered daughter who would make a suitable mistress for the Abbey. That would be fitting, indeed inevitable. But Annabelle Fortescue! He would be better off with herself. At least she was a real lady, not some jumped-up solicitor's daughter who was barely fit to marry Dick.

She went up to her bedchamber, slumped on to the edge of her bed, and sat repining. This summer, which had begun in such a blaze of glory, was rapidly turning into one of the worst since the year her mama had died and she had had to delay her wedding to Lyle Standish. Nothing was working out as she had hoped. It seemed the only well-matched pair in the parish were Dick and Sylvia Rafferty, and even they could not get on with their romance. She thought of Sylvester, not in the light of the precious letter in her pocket but as Dick saw him. Sylvester was too young for her, too superficial, too dandified. Harry hadn't a good word to say for him either. If she were perfectly honest with herself, she would admit she didn't care so much for him as for the entrée to the literary world she had long coveted.

Compared to Harry, he was a mere stripling. Her thoughts were easily diverted to Harry. She saw him again in her mind's eye, walking hand in hand with Sukey, carrying Snow Drop. He would not be allowed to run tame at Apple Hill if Annabelle nabbed him. Her ladyship would see to that! Harry had been a part of her life for as long as she could remember. He was always there, laughing, joking, cadging favors, and granting them, too, when she and Dick needed a wiser head to advise them. Oh, why couldn't things remain as they had been?

She blinked back the tears that pricked the back of her eyes and went to her toilet table to contrive a coiffure for the party. She would not wear the turban after all. She'd look like Sylvester's mama.

At six-thirty she and Dick went to say good night to Sukey, who always liked to see them arrayed in their finery when they were going out. Rosalind had drawn her hair into a nest of curls on top of her head and wore again her rose gown. Miss Rafferty, looking like Cinderella deprived of the ball, sat with Sukey reading her a story.

"You look very nice, Miss Lovelace," she said. "I hope you have a good time." Then with a shy glance at Dick, "And you too, Mr Lovelace."

Dick's lips clenched into a grimace. "Thank you, Miss Rafferty. I'm sorry you aren't coming with us. Demmed foolishness."

The trip to Croydon was made in near silence. They were as dispirited as if they were in a tumbrel on their way to the guillotine. Their spirits revived somewhat when they reached Fortescue's mansion. The flaming torches, the row of scarlet-clad footmen, and the canopy erected over the doorway were enough to bring a smile to Rosalind's lips. Really, it was too ridiculous! How Harry would stare!

Annabelle's gown of Olympian blue was all one could imagine and more in the way of ribbons, lace, ruchings, and silk flowers. The daring cut revealed her white shoulders, but one's eyes were more likely to be drawn to the sapphires around her neck. Sylvester sat beside her like a tame puppy. His supercilious manner had left him entirely. Annabelle greeted the Lovelaces with a chilly smile.

"How nice you look, Rosalind. I am becoming fond of that gown," she said, with a dismissing glance at the familiar garment. She merely nodded to Dick, before turning to address some comment to Sylvester. Sylvester smiled uneasily at Rosalind and murmured his greeting. The Lovelaces hurried on to speak to other guests and were soon sharing exclamations of astonishment at the canopy and conjecture as to the turtle soup to come. Miss Vickers's maid had got a look at the live creature and thought it looked very old and tough for eating.

Lord Harwell was one of the last to arrive. Rosalind had been waiting for him, and when she saw him, she gazed a long moment. How fine he looked compared to every other man in the room. His shirt points were not so high as some, his diamond not half the size of Fortescue's, but he had an air of dignity and of casual, unstudied charm that set him apart from the common herd.

He glanced quickly around the room and smiled at Rosalind when he saw her chatting to the Floods, on the far side of the room from Sylvester. Their eyes met and held, as if they shared something deep and important. Then he heard his name spoken and turned away.

Annabelle drew Harwell to her side and engaged him in some banter. Rosalind watched from the corner of her eye as the chit batted her fan, twitched at her necklace, preened her hair, laughed too loudly, and generally behaved as commonly as one expected.

When all the dinner guests had arrived and consumed a glass of very good sherry, a footman sounded a gong and Mrs Fortescue led the party in to dinner.

The guests invited to dinner were limited to two dozen, but the meal might have fed ten times the number. Lady Amanda Vaughan, the only titled female present, was placed at Mr Fortescue's right hand. Lord Harwell sat beside her. Annabelle sat beside him, with Sylvester on her other side, thus hogging the two most eligible catches at the party.

Rosalind and Dick were not seated below the salt, but they were not distinguished in any way from lesser guests. Annabelle divided her time between Sylvester and Harwell. Rosalind, seated farther down the board on the other side, had difficulty keeping an eye on her goings-on. A floral arrangement as big as a bathtub made vision difficult.

The turtle soup was a great triumph. Mrs Fortescue regaled her end of the table with the tale of the turtle's acquisition and preparation.

"Mr Fortescue had it brought down from the London market in a tub of water to keep it fresh, so you need not fear you'll get food poisoning from it. A deal of bother, but Belle had her little heart set on turtle soup. 'Tis all the crack in London, so she tells us. She had the receipt from Lady Dunston's chef."

Despite its strange taste, the guests felt compelled to clean their bowls and pronounce it the best turtle they had ever tasted. As it was the only one most of them had ever tasted, this was no lie.

Course followed course and remove followed remove until a glutton could not ask more. But still there was more. Desserts, six of them, and a savory followed. Whipped cream, fresh berries, all manner of dainty cakes and tarts were handed around by the footmen, and new plates placed on the groaning board on either side of the floral arrangement. Rosalind was not the only lady wondering what would become of all the leftovers. Even with every spare person in the village pressed into service, they could not consume all that went back to the kitchen.

All the work and money were deemed worthwhile when Harwell said at the meal's conclusion, "Prinny could not have done us more proud, Fortescue. A meal to remember."

A beaming Mrs Fortescue said, "Now, that is what I call a pretty compliment!" Mr Fortescue smiled his satisfaction, and Annabelle shot a spiteful little glance down the board to Rosalind.

The ladies escaped to the Red Saloon to sink, replete, on to the sofas and await the gentlemen. Annabelle waited to see where Rosalind sat, then went to her, but did not sit down.

"Lord Sylvester will have something to say to you later, Miss Lovelace," she said, with a triumphant smile, "and I shall have something to say to Dick." Before Rosalind could reply, she glided along to the other end of the room, leaving Miss Lovelace to wonder about a few things, not least why she had suddenly become

Miss Lovelace when she had been Roz for half a year, and even a premature Sis on a few occasions, when Annabelle was in good humor.

CHAPTER
NINETEEN

When the gentlemen joined the ladies, Harwell took up the empty seat Rosalind had been expecting Sylvester to occupy. Sylvester did not go to Annabelle at least, but sat with her mama. The smiles in that quarter suggested he was inventing compliments on the feast.

"I shall have to have a word with Cook," Harwell said. "I was planning only two courses and two removes for your farewell dinner. After this repast, I feel I ought to borrow Careme from Prinny and do the thing up properly."

"And all this for no special occasion either," Rosalind said. "Unless one can call Fortescue's thousand pounds to *Camena* a special occasion. The party must have cost twice that."

"Those sapphires Annabelle is sporting didn't come cheap either. Fortescue's pockets must be even deeper than I thought."

Rosalind noticed that he was looking at the sapphires. When his eyes wandered up to Annabelle's face, he smiled. There was no denying she was pretty. Why had Dick suggested Harwell should offer for her? Had he noticed some attraction between them that she had not? Harry was always sure to stand up with

Annabelle at all the assemblies. Rosalind had always taken it as a sort of compliment to Dick, but perhaps there was more to it than that. A strange fluttering began in her chest. She wanted to tease him, but no words came. Surely he was not admiring the hussy? Before more was said, the company invited for the dancing party began to pour in, and soon Mrs Fortescue announced that the musicians were ready in the ballroom.

Sylvester went to Annabelle then and offered her his arm. Did it without thinking, as if it were a settled thing. As if he were her acknowledged escort. Harwell shot a questioning look at Rosalind, but she didn't see it. She was busy rationalizing that as Fortescue's houseguest, Sylvester was merely being polite.

"Looks like you are stuck with me," Harwell said, and rose to offer her his arm. She took it silently, feeling embarrassed in front of him after having boasted about Sylvester. Harwell sensed her *gêne* and said, "What's the matter, Roz? Don't give her the satisfaction of seeing your nose is out of joint."

"I am just wondering what Dick thinks of this performance," she replied.

"Better than Covent Garden. And it's free."

The first dance was a minuet. Little talk was necessary and no real conversation possible. Such words as the movements of the dance allowed were about the music. Rosalind said the London musicians were very good. Harwell replied that they were the group used at the best London balls. Sylvester must have put her on to them.

178

Her annoyance was slightly relieved when Sylvester came to her for the second set. He was as friendly as ever. He made a few jokes about the elaborate meal. He asked if she had had his letter and gave a few more details about the matters discussed in it. Nothing appeared to have changed between them. Yet she knew she could never care for him enough to marry him. Even if he professed undying devotion and a title besides, she could not do it.

Before they parted, he said in a conspiratorial way, "I have to talk to you in private, Roz. Fortescue is going to make the announcement. Meet me in the conservatory after. Come alone."

It was a curious request. She agreed to it as much out of curiosity as anything. Fortescue's announcement, she assumed, had to do with his joint venture with Sylvester in *Camena*. When their dance was over, Sylvester darted back to Mr Fortescue's side. Annabelle joined him. The little group proceeded to the front of the ballroom. Fortescue had a word with the musicians, they set aside their instruments, and he mounted the musicians' raised platform. The room fell silent, every eye turned on him.

He began a rambling speech, first about *Camena* and his joining the board of directors. As the words flowed on, the name Lord Sylvester occurred with increasing frequency, veering from his native genius in having a marquess for a papa and writing and editing poetry to more personal praise.

"A young gentleman of wit, character, and integrity who has become like a son to me. I am proud to announce that he soon will be. My daughter, Annabelle, has accepted his offer of marriage."

The announcement was followed by a few seconds of stunned silence while this incredible fact was digested. Into the hush came the words "Good God!" issued in no quiet voice by Lady Amanda, followed by a raucous laugh. Then the dam of silence broke and a babble of sound rose all around. Rosalind scarcely heard it for the ringing in her ears as she stood, pale and staring.

She was dimly aware of the crowd thrusting forward to offer their best wishes to the couple and Fortescue. Dick was suddenly at her side.

"Thank God that's over!" he said, in heartfelt accents. "Let us go home and tell Miss Rafferty."

"No! It will be noticed if we leave now. We must congratulate them." As she peered around the room, she noticed several pairs of eyes regarding Dick in a questioning way. Hardly surprising as no rescinding of Annabelle's engagement to him had been made.

"Very well, let us get it over with then."

He took Rosalind's elbow and jostled her forward. Over a few heads he called, "Congratulations, milord. Every happiness, Annabelle."

Annabelle lifted her head and cast a gloating, triumphant smile at the Lovelaces. "Sorry, Dick," she said. "Too kind of you. I'll see that you get your little engagement ring back." Rosalind noticed then that she was not wearing it, but she was not wearing Sylvester's ring either. Her third finger was bare of any ring.

She was unaware that her new fiancé was looking at Rosalind with a conspiratorial grin lifting his lips.

180

Rosalind despised him at that moment. There was no public shame to her in the announcement. The neighbors knew nothing of her romance with Sylvester. Only Harry and Dick knew she was expecting an offer. This was humiliating, but it was not what caused her anger.

It was that sly smile Sylvester cast in her direction. She was taken with the notion that he had no intention of marrying Annabelle. It was some stunt to get more money out of Fortescue. Could he really be that lacking in character? She remembered his request that she meet him in the conservatory after the announcement. Her first instinct was to ignore the meeting and go home. A second thought changed her mind. She would go to the conservatory and discover exactly his true intentions regarding Annabelle. And if they were as she suspected, she would ring a peal over the wretch that would be heard in London. London! She could not possibly go there under his auspices now.

Deep in thought, she paid little heed to the surrounding melée. When she shook herself back to attention, she heard a few friends commiserating with Dick, whose high spirits sounded false, but were, in fact, genuine. It was embarrassment that made him laugh too loud and utter such ill-bred inanities as "Better him than me!"

Overcome with it all, Rosalind turned to leave the room and found herself confronted with Harwell. He wore a small scowl. She knew it was anger on her behalf, and knew, too, that the gentle hand placed on her arm was a gesture of support and genuine affection.

He looked like the only sane, rational person in the room. Her anger with Sylvester and Annabelle dissipated like dew in the morning sun. How could Dick think for a moment that Harry would ever offer for Annabelle?

"Shall I take you home?" was all he said.

It was like him to completely ignore the shame and ill-bred folly of this night and try to spare her feelings.

"Dick and I will be leaving in a moment," she said, and added simply, "Thank you, Harry."

"You are better off without him."

"I know. It's all right. I am not going to do anything foolish. I just want a word with Sylvester. He asked me to meet him in the conservatory. To apologize, I expect."

They walked to the edge of the room. "He's left it a bit late. Annabelle's doing, no doubt. She wanted to stun the world with her announcement. How is Dick taking it?"

"He's delighted."

"Good."

Rosalind wanted a few moments to collect her thoughts before meeting Sylvester. "Why don't you have a word with Dick?" she suggested.

Harry squeezed her fingers, gave her an encouraging smile, and left.

She went to the conservatory to wait. Wrapped up in her thoughts, she was oblivious of the swaying palms and pungent scent from the lemon trees around her, but she did appreciate the silence. She just wanted to be away from the crowd for some private brooding.

Now that the shock was over, she wondered what Sylvester was going to say. Perhaps she had misjudged him and he truly cared for Annabelle and intended to marry her. He just wanted to apologize, or settle some details of her remove to London.

As if she would go there now! Sylvester could no longer be her escort when he was engaged to Annabelle, and she had no wish to crash society on her own. If Sylvester made some token gesture of showing her around, Annabelle would be at his side, making a vulgar show of herself. No, it would not do. She would remain at Apple Hill. For tonight, she would hear what he had to say, and tell him she was not going to London. No doubt he would be relieved.

When all this was settled in her mind, she began to stroll around the conservatory, suddenly aware of the cloying perfume of the flowers and the moist warmth of the air. Knowing that Sylvester could not dash off the minute after the announcement, she settled in for a wait.

CHAPTER
TWENTY

After half an hour, Rosalind heard light footsteps entering the conservatory. She rose from the wrought-iron bench on which she had been resting to greet Sylvester. When he espied her, he rushed forward, both arms reaching for her.

"Rosalind! Sorry I am so late coming to you, but we must keep the old boy in curl. You won't believe how much he's putting into *Camena*. Five thousand! And that on top of Annabelle's dowry!"

Her lips pinched in distaste. She realized at once that he had drunk more wine than he should, which would account for his blunt words. Sylvester was usually more discreet. At this close range, she could see his eyes looked glazed, and his smile was slack. As his words sank in, she realized that Sylvester did intend to marry Annabelle at least.

"You sound as if that's the only reason you're marrying Annabelle," she charged, annoyed with him.

He uttered a happy laugh. "What other conceivable reason could there be? The wench is impossible. Really, the vulgarity of this party! If any of my friends had seen it, I'd be ashamed."

"Do you not plan to introduce your fiancée to your friends?"

He frowned. "I must eventually, after I have smartened her up."

"But you are only marrying her for her papa's money?"

His two hands seized hers. "My dear, of course. You know I would sacrifice anything for *Camena*. It won't make any difference to us. Is that why you've been glaring at me so fiercely all evening? I am still mad for you, Rosalind. With all Fortescue's blunt, I'll be able to set you up in a finer style than that flat on Glasshouse Street. We'll want someplace discreet. Annabelle knows about the Glasshouse flats." He gave a lecherous little laugh. "We won't want your brother and neighbors to know what is going on either, eh? I think Harwell is becoming a little jealous."

Rosalind just stared, beyond speech, almost beyond belief. There was no ignoring his meaning. She had first thought the "I'm still mad for you" was a preamble to some poetic denunciation of love for art, but that "set you up" left her in no doubt at all. He wanted her for his mistress. That was all he had ever wanted.

"Are you insane?" she demanded.

"Just a little tipsy with joy — and love for you, my darling!"

On this speech, he pulled her into his arms and tried to plant his wine-soaked lips on hers. Caught off his guard, he was easy to push away. One hard shove sent him flying into a lemon tree, sharp with thorns.

"It would take more than all of Fortescue's blunt to make me have anything to do with you, milord. I would not marry you for all the tea in China, and I would certainly never even consider such a repulsive creature for a lover!"

"Harwell won't have you back, if that's what you have been up to, trying to make your old lover jealous by using me."

"Lover?" she exclaimed. "He was never my lover. We are friends. I come to think Annabelle Fortescue is too good for you. At least her vulgarity is not ill intentioned, like your conniving. She is only trying to impress you. You are trying to deceive her."

As she ranted, shaking her finger at him in a fine fit of temper, Sylvester scrambled out of the tree's embrace. "What a delightful surprise!" he said, arching his eyebrows in approval. "I never guessed you had a temper. Jealousy has heated up that English sangfroid. I like a hot-blooded lady."

His arms went around her, pulling her against him, as he tried for a kiss. Although half-drunk, he was still stronger than she was. Rosalind pushed against his shoulders and began looking about for a rock or a broom to use as a weapon.

She was still Sylvester's captive when Lord Harwell came pelting forward with blood in his eyes. He looked ready to kill poor Sylvester. Harwell hauled him off by the padding of his shoulders, dropped him to the floor, and raised a fist to land him a facer.

Sylvester rallied enough to raise his two fists and began prancing about like a bruiser. As he feinted a few blows into the air, he said, "This has nothing to do with you, Harwell!"

"On the contrary! I take it very much amiss when someone propositions the lady I am going to marry."

Sylvester's shocked "Marry?" was overborne by Rosalind's "Don't be foolish, Harry."

Harwell landed Sylvester a poke in the eye that sent him flying into the lemon tree. A ripe lemon, loosened by the shaking, fell and landed on his head. Harwell reached down to pull him up and hit him again.

"Don't bother, Harry. He's drunk as a Dane," Rosalind said.

Harwell gave a "Bah!" of disgust and threw him back into the arms of the thorny lemon tree.

Annabelle, alert to any deviations from devotion by her new fiancé, had soon followed him to the conservatory. She came screeching forward to rescue her beloved. She cradled him in her arms, crooning endearments. Then she lifted her head and said to Harwell in the grande dame style, "Perhaps it would be best if you leave now, milord."

Rosalind suddenly felt sorry for the chit. "Annabelle, you can't marry this wretch!" she said.

Annabelle tossed her curls. "You think I didn't know what he was up to? I saw him speak to you. Why do you think I followed him here? I would have made short shrift of you, miss! And anyone else who thinks to lead my Sylvester astray." She turned to Sylvester. "Naughty boy!" she added archly, and gave his chin a pinch. "Come on, get up, Sylvester, before Papa comes."

She hauled her fiancé up from the gardening pot and began to brush leaves and dust from his jacket. "We'll have to put something on that eye," she scolded.

"Forgive me, my sweet," Sylvester said. "A little too much champagne."

Rosalind just looked at Harwell in bewilderment. He shook his head and rolled his eyes ceilingward.

Annabelle was not likely to overlook a new match, even in the midst of such chaos. She looked up at Rosalind and said, "So you have finally nabbed Harwell. Congratulations, Roz."

Rosalind's "No indeed!" was overridden by Harwell's, "Thank you, ma'am." He took a firm grip on Rosalind's arm and led her out before Annabelle could demand clarification.

Annabelle came pelting after them. "About that flat on Glasshouse Street, Roz. I doubt you would like it. Some of the tenants are no better than they should be. It is exactly what my Aunt Venetia is looking for, however."

Rosalind swallowed her laughter at the unintentional slur on the unknown Aunt Venetia. "Then by all means, let her have it. She will help you keep an eye on your husband."

"Exactly! And, Roz — you'll tell Dick how sorry I am. But really, you know, the son of a marquess! I don't have to tell *you*," she said, casting an arch smile from Rosalind to Harwell, as if the two ladies had conspired together to each nab a title for herself.

"I understand," Rosalind said. She felt sorry for Annabelle, and unutterably happy for Dick's deliverance. She even felt a little sorry for Sylvester. If he thought he was marrying easy money, he was much mistaken.

"And about *Camena* — I fear, under the circumstances, it will be impossible for us to continue publishing your little rhymes," Annabelle said. "We want the magazine to have a more serious tone. Papa will handle the administration, leaving my Sylvester free to write his sublime poetry."

"That is quite all right," Harwell said. "*Blackwood's* has made a better offer." He bowed formally. "Good evening, Lady Sylvester," he said, and walked off with Rosalind, who was downcast to hear her publishing career was over.

"Just reminding her of the title. Wouldn't want her to change her mind," he said, when they were beyond earshot. "About *Blackwood's*, Roz."

"I know. It was merely to annoy her and save my face."

"Yes, but I might be able to twist someone's arm."

"What a wretched muddle. I feel sorry for everyone. Annabelle's match was made in the devil's workshop."

"No, purchased at Vanity Fair. The lady wants a title. The gentleman — and I use both words loosely — wants her blunt. They deserve each other."

"Let us find Dick and get out of this abominable place."

"I'll take you home."

Rosalind did not forget Harwell's announcement that he planned to marry her. When he didn't mention it again, she assumed he had spoken rashly in the heat of the moment to defend her honor, or perhaps just to give him an excuse to poke Sylvester in the eye. At least he had not heard Sylvester's charge that he had been her lover.

"We had best have a word with Annabelle first," she said, glancing at him uncertainly.

"Afraid she'll make our announcement for us?"

"You can't expect her to keep such a prize piece of news to herself. She doesn't know you were joking."

"Who said I was joking?"

She peered at him in the darkness. "Well, you only said it to have an excuse to hit Sylvester."

"I own that was one reason. The desire to beat him has been growing over the past weeks," he replied. He looked at her, waiting for her to ask what other reason he might have.

She murmured, "You are not the only one. Dick can't abide him either. As to your offering for me, however, that is too much to ask of friendship."

As she spoke, she was looking around for Dick. Perhaps Annabelle would not tell anyone what Harwell had said. Sylvester's eye would very likely be darkening by now, and she would be busy concealing it from Mr Fortescue and the guests.

Dick came from the ballroom to meet them. "Are we off?" he said to Rosalind.

"Yes, let us go. Thank you for — everything, Harry."

"We'll talk tomorrow. You'll want to think about it." His dark eyes gazed into hers for a longish moment, then he pressed her trembling fingers to his lips before leaving.

190

"This is a night I wouldn't want to have to live through again," Dick said. He called for their carriage, and they drove home. Rosalind wished they might repeat the silence of their trip to the party, but it was not to be.

She told him briefly what had happened in the conservatory, before he heard some worse version. She omitted only Sylvester's hint that Harwell and she had been lovers. Heaven only knew what Annabelle would make of that if Sylvester told her.

"Sure Harwell didn't mean it, about offering for you?" he asked.

"Of course."

Dick was so enraptured to be free of his shackles that he soon forgot Rosalind's doings and babbled like a boy. The name Miss Rafferty was not spoken, but her presence was felt lurking behind every word.

"I hope Annabelle will be happy. Marriage is a very good thing, by and large. A fellow reaches a certain age and wants to settle down. I daresay that is why I ever offered for her in the first place. I see now she is not at all the sort of lady for me. I want someone quieter, who won't upset the household and want to be darting off to London, squandering a fortune on gowns and gewgaws. Some nice, quiet girl who will get along well with Sukey."

All Rosalind had to do was nod, and he continued, leaving her free to ponder her own position. "You'll want to think about it," Harry had said, referring, of course, to his announcement that he planned to make her his wife.

Rosalind had no doubt in her mind that she wanted to marry him. The feeling had been buried deep inside her for years, and it had been growing in strength all spring. It was only the unlikelihood of his ever offering that had kept the hope suppressed. What bedeviled her now was whether he really meant it. She knew she wouldn't sleep a wink for thinking how lovely it would be if he did.

CHAPTER
TWENTY-ONE

Rosalind's night was as restless as she knew it would be. She gave scarcely a thought to the interruption in her career. She would continue writing for her own pleasure, and submit her work to *Blackwood's* and the *Edinburgh Review* and the *Examiner* and any other literary magazine she could think of. If the poems were any good, they would find a publisher eventually. She wouldn't pretend she was a man either. She was a little known now, after being puffed up in *Camena*.

The greater quandary was to do with her relationship with Harry. She could think of no greater happiness than to marry him and go on living next door to Apple Hill. She would still get to London. Harwell enjoyed the liveliness of the Season. He enjoyed it very much — too much. Would he try Sylvester's stunts on his bride? She had not Annabelle's tolerance for infidelity. That was one thing she must get clear with him — if he truly wanted to marry her.

Dick was radiant at breakfast. He could scarcely control his smiles.

"Since the day is so fine, Sylvia and I are going for a ride with Sukey," he announced, the minute she sat down. No more "Miss Rafferty" was necessary. "Sylvia will ride the spare mount. You need not fear she plans to usurp your nag, Roz. I offered her the use of Lady. The spare hack is on its last legs. She wouldn't hear of using Lady."

Dick had offered Miss Rafferty the use of her mount, and without asking her. Rosalind noticed that already Miss Rafferty was being placed above her, as was only right, but it still hurt a little. She knew it was but the first of many little unintentional slights. Miss Rafferty was a modest creature, but even she would want to be mistress of her own home.

"I expect Annabelle's announcement will be in the local journal today," was his next speech.

"Oh, certainly, and in the London journals by tomorrow."

He spooned a dollop of strawberry jam on to his toast and said nonchalantly, "How long do you figure a fellow must wait to announce a new engagement, after he's been jilted?"

"You and Miss Rafferty ought to wait a few weeks, Dick."

"Deuce take it, what makes you think I was talking about myself?"

"Just a guess," she said, shaking her head.

"I haven't even asked her yet — but she is a darling, ain't she?"

"I like her very much."

"And there's no fear she'd try to freeze you out of your home either. She ain't that sort. We shall all be merry as grigs. You can write a poem about it."

As soon as he had gulped his gammon and eggs, he rose and went to order the horses saddled. Sukey and Miss Rafferty soon came downstairs, outfitted for riding.

"I expect I shall fall off," Miss Rafferty said, glancing shyly at Rosalind. "I've never ridden before. Lady Syon gave me this riding habit when she had a new one made. I had planned to make a walking suit out of it."

"You look very nice," Dick said. "We'll go through the spinney. It is soft falling there. You'll get the hang of it in no time." As he spoke, he ushered Miss Rafferty out, with a proprietary and unbusinesslike grip on her elbow.

"We'll do our lessons this afternoon, Miss Sukey," Sylvia called over her shoulder.

Sukey gave a very knowing look. "April and May," she said, handing Snow Drop to Rosalind. "Take good care of her for me. She doesn't like me riding. Sandy will go with me, though. Snow Drop's just for fun. She can't keep the pace."

Snow Drop hopped down from Rosalind's arms and disappeared under the table. Sukey went scampering off after the others. No assuming of airs was necessary with Miss Rafferty. They left via the kitchen and the back door. Rosalind picked up Snow Drop again and stroked her neck, thinking of Sylvester and Harry.

She waited a quarter of an hour and when still Harwell hadn't come, she took her lap writing desk into the garden. She was sitting on the wicker bench in the shade of the tall lilac bushes when Harwell came strolling forth from the stable, where he had left his mount.

He was dressed more formally than usual, wearing a proper cravat in lieu of a kerchief. He wore a sober face to match the cravat. Not the face of a man in love, Rosalind decided as she watched his approach. That cravat hinted at London. He was going to London to save her the embarrassment of meeting with him for a few days. He already regretted his rashness of the night before. She would put him out of his misery at once. She owed that much to her oldest and dearest friend.

"No need to look like an undertaker," she said, offering him her hand and smiling fondly. "I don't plan to hold you to your rash announcement, sir."

Harwell held on to her hand, drawing her up from her seat. "Not you!" he said, with an answering smile and a little shake of his head. "You are not a Miss Fortescue after all, to be snatching at a title."

"And from a gentleman who is much too fond of the ladies besides," she added. She could not suppress a little frown to realize her dream was to come to naught.

He leapt on it. "Is that why you are refusing me? I have sown my wild oats long ago, Roz."

"Yes, a whole two weeks ago, if memory serves. You told me right in this garden two weeks ago that you had enjoyed some delightful flirtations in London."

"I lied," he said, with a deep, penetrating gaze. "The Season was just another dreary round of simpering debs, no different from the debs last year. I am too old for schoolgirls. I need a real woman to share my life with me. That was the day I realized I had outgrown

196

flirting and was ready to settle down. I wondered then why I had bothered with London this year, when you were here all the time."

The breath caught in her lungs. "I have been here two and a half decades, Harry," she reminded him.

"And it took Sylvester to make me realize I have loved you all the time. We never realize what we have, until we are in danger of losing it." He tried to gather her into his arms. She stepped back and stared at him.

"You overheard Sylvester last night," she said. "That's why you're here. But I'm sure he won't tell anyone, Harry. He cannot have told Annabelle, or she would have thrown it in my face. We would have heard the words 'bit of muslin'!"

"I didn't overhear it, actually. But he thought I had when I called on Fortescue this morning. Sylvester waylaid me. He was trembling like a leaf. He thought I had come to offer him a challenge. He won't mention it. I put the fear of the Lord into him."

"What on earth did you want to see him about in the first place?"

"I didn't go to see him. I had an appointment with Fortescue. We are cooperating in building a new block of flats in Croydon. He's a shrewd businessman. He screwed the mortgage rate down a whole percent. But I didn't come to talk business, Roz." He took a deep breath, swallowed twice, and said, "I came to ask you to marry me."

"You don't have to do this, Harry. I'm not going to London to make a fool of myself. I plan to stay on here with Dick and Sukey."

"The Abbey is not that far away. You can still do Dick's accounts if that —"

"No! It's not that."

"What is it you dislike? I can change," he said simply, with even an air of uncertainty.

Tears dimmed her eyes. "I don't want you to change. Well, not much," she said in a husky voice.

"Then what —"

"Oh, Harry!"

The way she said it, in a voice throbbing with emotion, was a cry from the very depths of her heart. He gazed at her for a long moment with a fixed, penetrating eye and lips lightly curved in delight, while storing up this precious image in memory for all time. This was the woman he loved, had always loved, and he trembled to think how close he had come to losing her.

Then his arms reached instinctively for her, and she went into them with the joyous satisfaction of a long-delayed dream finally coming true. His arms tightened inexorably around her, pressing her to his heart as his lips found hers for a deep, lingering kiss, which felt as if the other half of himself had finally come home, making him whole. They clung to each other with a fierce tenderness while the kiss soared to passion.

In the lilac bushes overhead, the blossoms were gone, but it felt like blossom time in his heart.

Also available in ISIS Large Print:

Lie by Moonlight

Amanda Quick

During an investigation into a woman's death, gentleman thief turned private inquiry agent Ambrose Wells finds himself at Aldwick Castle — in the midst of chaos. The building is in flames. Men are dead. And a woman and four young girls are fleeing on horseback.

A confirmed loner, Ambrose nevertheless finds himself taking Miss Concordia Glade and her young charges under his wing. With their lives at risk, he insists they must remain in hiding until he is able to unravel the truth behind their recent imprisonment at the castle.

Concordia has never met anyone like Ambrose Wells before. He is bold, clever and inscrutable — even to the perceptive gaze of a professional teacher such as herself. He is also her only hope of protection from the unscrupulous men who are after them — powerful, shadowy figures who will stop at nothing to get what they want.

ISBN 0-7531-7457-X (hb)
ISBN 0-7531-7458-8 (pb)

An Infamous Army

Georgette Heyer

In 1815, under the aegis of the Army of Occupation, Brussels is the gayest town in Europe. And the widow Lady Barbara Childe, renowned for being as outrageous as she is beautiful, is at the centre of all that is fashionable and light-hearted. When she meets Charles Audley, the elegant and handsome aide-de-camp to the great Duke of Wellington himself, her joie de vivre knows no bounds — until the eve of the fateful Battle of Waterloo . . .

ISBN 0-7531-7413-8 (hb)
ISBN 0-7531-7414-6 (pb)

Petticoat Rebellion

Joan Smith

For Abbie Fairchild, an art teacher and aspiring artist, the opportunity to spend a week at Penfel Hall with its grand art gallery is a dream come true.

But the field trip takes a scandalous turn when the eccentric dowager Lady Penfel shamelessly orchestrates a petticoat rebellion, encouraging young ladies in Abbie's care to make fools of themselves over various rogues. For why should gentlemen have all the fun and ladies none?

Why indeed, Abbie wonders, when she meets the devilishly attractive Lord Penfel. Logic dictates she's out of her depth with this practised lothario. But the heart is not ruled by logic . . .

ISBN 0-7531-7451-0 (hb)
ISBN 0-7531-7452-9 (pb)

A Christmas Gambol

Joan Smith

The gentleman was a dyed-in-the-wool romantic. But he had much to learn about love!

When aspiring writer Cicely Caldwell agrees to pose as the anonymous lady author of the vastly popular "Chaos Is Come Again", she is calculating that such a pretence will gain her entrée into the literary circles that might give a lift to her own writing career. But she is certain that the impossibly handsome Lord Montaigne is not telling the truth when claiming the book to be the work of his aunt. Unravelling the truth leads Cicely directly to the man whose outward cynicism cannot hide his true romantic nature . . . on or off the page.

ISBN 0-7531-7249-6 (hb)
ISBN 0-7531-7250-X (pb)

The Kissing Bough

Joan Smith

A delightful Regency romance from the author of The Savage Lord Griffin

Jane Ramsay was thrilled to receive an invitation to spend a country Christmas with Nicholas, heir to Lord Goderich, who was — by his own proclamation — ready to settle down at last. Yet her hopes of a proposal fall flat — the house party was being held in honour of his angelic bride-to-be. But since it is high time for Jane to choose a husband and Nick's friend Pelham seems as good as any, she proceeds to accept his attentions. But if the jealousy in Nick's eyes wasn't proof enough of his hidden affection for her, then surely his embrace under the kissing bough will upset everyone's best laid plans . . .

ISBN 0-7531-7077-9 (hb)
ISBN 0-7531-7078-7 (pb)

ISIS publish a wide range of books in large print, from fiction to biography. Any suggestions for books you would like to see in large print or audio are always welcome. Please send to the Editorial Department at:

ISIS Publishing Limited
7 Centremead
Osney Mead
Oxford OX2 0ES

A full list of titles is available free of charge from:

Ulverscroft Large Print Books Limited

(UK)
The Green
Bradgate Road, Anstey
Leicester LE7 7FU
Tel: (0116) 236 4325

(Australia)
P.O. Box 314
St Leonards
NSW 1590
Tel: (02) 9436 2622

(USA)
P.O. Box 1230
West Seneca
N.Y. 14224-1230
Tel: (716) 674 4270

(Canada)
P.O. Box 80038
Burlington
Ontario L7L 6B1
Tel: (905) 637 8734

(New Zealand)
P.O. Box 456
Feilding
Tel: (06) 323 6828

Details of **ISIS** complete and unabridged audio books are also available from these offices. Alternatively, contact your local library for details of their collection of **ISIS** large print and unabridged audio books.